THE ROSE FANCIER

OLGA MASTERS

THE ROSE FANCIER

University of Queensland Press
ST LUCIA • LONDON • NEW YORK

First published 1988 by University of Queensland Press
Box 42, St Lucia, Queensland, Australia

Typeset by University of Queensland Press
Printed in Australia by The Book Printer, Melbourne

Distributed in the UK and Europe by University of Queensland Press
Dunhams Lane, Letchworth, Herts. SG6 1LF England

Distributed in the USA and Canada by University of Queensland Press
250 Commercial Street, Manchester, NH 03101 USA

This publication has been funded by The Australian
Bicentennial Authority to celebrate Australia's Bicentenary
in 1988

 Creative writing program assisted by
the Literary Arts Board of the Australia
Council, the Federal Government's arts
funding and advisory body

Cataloguing in Publication Data

National Library of Australia

Masters, Olga, 1919–1986.
    The rose fancier.
    I. Title.
A823'.3

British Library (data available)

Library of Congress

Masters, Olga, 1919–1986.
    The rose fancier.
    Bibliography: p.
    Includes index.
    I. Title.
PR9619.3.M289R6   1988   823'.914   88-4755
ISBN 0 7022 2080 9

Contents

Acknowledgments

Some of these stories have been published before: "The Boy with Two Birthdays" in *Australian Short Stories*; "The Rose Fancier" in *Antipodes* (USA); and "Brown and Green Giraffes" in *The Babe is Wise*, edited by Lyn Harwood, Bruce Pascoe and Paula White (Melbourne: Pascoe Publishing Pty Ltd, 1987).

Publisher's Note

When Olga Masters died in September 1986 she was still at work on this collection. She had chosen the book's name, outlined the sequence of stories, and prepared final drafts of eight stories: "The Boy with Two Birthdays", "A Stupid Child", "Home Sick", "Here Blue", "Whatever Pa Says", "A Lovely Day", "Brown and Green Giraffes" and "The Rose Fancier". However, nine other stories, plus a fragment of a tenth, were still in early draft form.

The presentation of the early drafts was rough, but the storylines, scenes, characters and dialogue were all in place or at least sketched in, and UQP and the Masters family thought that the stories could, with editing, be combined with the eight finished drafts in a book not too dissimilar from the one Olga had planned.

Editorial alterations to the nine early drafts were restricted, as much as possible, to the kinds of corrections Olga herself had approved in the editing of previous books. Some scenes were clarified, but little was deleted and nothing added.

UQP wishes to thank the members of Olga Masters's family for their assistance and support during the production of this book. We also wish to thank Dorothy Jones of the University of Wollongong for her invaluable advice.

The Boy with Two Birthdays

Leo was in the middle of the thirteen McGovern children and the one born on January the first, 1888.

They lived on land selected by Leo's grandparents, who had migrated from Ireland about the middle of the century.

Because the time of his birth was the easiest to remember, Leo should have been the one McGovern to get his birthdate right. However for a long time there was confusion, for a sister was born at the end of the same year and died of diphtheria when she was five. Patrick and Sarah McGovern had put the date of Leo's birth forward, ashamed to have two children born in the same year. After they recovered from the loss of the little girl they were pleased they could now revert to Leo's proper age. But he had already started school, so he had one age for those records and another for home.

"Are you seven or eight?" (or "eight or nine" and so on) was constantly asked of Leo by the younger children. Leo began to look upon himself as an oddity, until Patrick at the big meal table, eating hogget chops and damper cooked on a camp oven, explained his good fortune in having the choice of two ages.

"Even Jesus only got one," he said with a big wink to Sarah who was seated (at last) at the corner closest to the fireplace where the camp oven hung, so that she could keep an eye on the new lot of chops jumping and spitting, ready for another serve to the older McGoverns, herself excluded. She was, she said, content with one serve, and had actually cooked up a little heap of trimmings which she ate, leaving the fat from them to cook the rest. "That's the one thing we should see to, Mother," Patrick said with another wink, causing Sarah to giggle pinkly into the neck of her dress. "We haven't got one born at Christmas."

"Thirteen of you!" (He crossed himself for the dead Beatrice.) "And none in December."

"So far." His wink was so large it screwed his face up and moved his big bushy beard.

Sarah, dipping her head even deeper into her neck, wished she could look disapproving. The blood tingling on her cheeks tingled around her thighs as well.

In the middle of December the fourteenth child was born. It lived but Sarah didn't. Patrick's old parents who farmed half the selection carried their belongings to their son's place and left their old shack to fall down. The going was rough, through salt and dog bush, great trees tangled to their tops with vines, sometimes shutting out the sun, ant hills and swamps, creek beds overgrown with blackberries. McGovern carried a chaff bag full of bedding with some plates and cups rolled inside, and his wife brought the basket Patrick had slept in as a baby, filled with their clothing, the last of their flour, sugar and tea and some jars of melon jam in her preserving pan under her other arm. It was a five mile walk with no tracks for a horse and dray although the McGoverns always talked about making some. Now it would not be necessary; the old couple would end their days with Patrick and the children.

He was their only child and old Mrs McGovern blamed Sarah not Patrick for the great tribe of children they had, as if it had taken certain skills to limit her own family to one. In fact the reason for barrenness settling in was attributed to a tipped womb, according to the bush nurse who attended Patrick's birth, Mrs McGovern having admitted to a feeling "down below", not actually a pain, rather as if something internal had jaws that refused to close. The nurse suggested attempts at straightening the organ, but Mrs Govern was against it, the stretched jaw feeling could continue; weighed against a dozen children it was the more acceptable.

The stone veranda along one side of Patrick's house had been laid by Patrick and the children old enough at the time to help. It was cool to bare feet at the height of summer, and any sharp edges were worn smooth by the feet rubbing away the burn of chilblains in winter.

On this December day the feet were burying into crevices looking for added relief, for the sun had been particularly fierce from early morning. Patrick and the children were lined up watching for the bush to part and give them the elder McGoverns. Only the eldest girl, Frances, sat on the edge holding the new baby, Noel. He was wrapped in a woollen shawl despite the heat. The exposed side of his face was a reddish tan colour, the frowning forehead raising minute eyebrows even in sleep, and the small mouth drawn into a circle making it even smaller. Frances stroked the cheek with a finger, ruffling the down still there from birth. A yell from the others made Frances jump though not the child, which she bound more tightly in her arms, rocking him while the others leapt about the stones, shrieking that the grandparents had come. Most of them ran to meet the old pair, adding to their burden by flinging arms around them and dragging on their load.

Three-year-old Cassie, a favourite of the grand-mother's, pulled the old woman down by the shoulders and straddled her hip, clinging there while she straightened up, unsteady after the long walk, nearly choking with the stranglehold on her throat. The older ones took her basket and the knitted rug from her shoulders, the easiest place to carry it although she sweltered under its weight and was scarlet of face.

She removed Cassie's arms to talk to Patrick, and Cassie clung harder to her shoulders and bound herself to her grandmother's waist with her thin little legs.

"Father Casey rode over just 'fore we left.

"He was on his way here, but seein' as we were comin' he asked for you to make a coffin for a young Coady, the sickly one."

Patrick, overcome, sat suddenly on his haunches. He had built the little church at Mogo, felling the trees and adzing the slabs with the help of the big boys, Kevin and Lennie. He made the coffins when local people died, (though not those of his little daughter or Sarah), but he went pale at the request as if a kind of remission had ended and the torment had returned. He rubbed his bare arms, hanging from the armholes of an old dark grey flannel, and all of the children looked soberly and wistfully at him, before some turned their faces away, unable to bear the sight of his.

Leo was chosen to ride with Patrick to take the coffin to the Coadys.

"The boy with the two birthdays!" Patrick decided, in good spirits again, having made a good job of the coffin. He was eating boiled beef and potatoes this time, with his mother at the corner of the table where Sarah used to sit. A place had been made for old Mr McGovern between Kevin and Alice, the second eldest girl, and those were the only changes since Sarah had died. Mrs McGovern made nice light currant dumplings, and she was all set to jump up and throw them in the water bubbling in her preserving pan.

The last of the potato was being scraped off the plates and piled on thick slices of bread to be eaten with green tomato pickle, very tart because sugar was a precious commodity used sparingly even for jam and forbidden in tea.

Leo could hardly believe he was the one to go. The ride was a long one, the Coadys had a place in a fold of Brown Mountain, a great blanket flung down from the sky, the top impregnable, the last two or three folds yielding reluctantly under the axes of the sturdy men making farms and raising families in homes of slab walls, earth floors and bark roofs in the beginning. When a few good seasons came in succession the farmers (Coady was one) rode to Patrick to ask him to replace the bark with shingles and lay one of his timber floors cut from the great cedar trees, leaving stumps as big as dining tables where little Coadys sat while their father ploughed around them.

Patrick felt a shameful sense of excitement at returning to Coadys, the first visit since he had built them a veranda on the eastern side of the house. Above the currant dumpling on his plate, his face creased gently with pleasure at the memory of Mrs Coady pulling out a rocking chair to sit and rock on the new boards, barely giving Patrick time to stow his saw and hammer and tin of nails in his hessian bag for the ride home. The Coady girls had fought with each other for the honour of giving

the veranda its first sweep, sending the sawdust flying
onto the ground where fowls picked, necks jerking level
with the boards, dull eyes blinking the question whether
to hop onto them.

"Dare you!" cried a thin red-haired Coady, flaying
one with a broom and sending it squawking down the
hill. Mrs Coady rocked on, dreaming of a fence around
the house, making it possible for her to grow the shy
flowers of her mother's garden in England.

The fence was still not up when Leo rode up with the
coffin.

Alone.

The Coadys lined the veranda, the rocking chair there
empty. None were crying. Even from a good distance,
his horse pulling hard up a steep slope leading to the
house, Leo could see the faces. Even the mother's wore
an expression of relief that he had come. Some eyes exchanged this relief, avoiding the mother's though,
respecting her sorrow above their own. Leo pulled his
horse up by a giant gum a few yards from the house. He
was unsure about dismounting, for he was on Patrick's
horse, a quivery golden-brown mare Patrick had broken
in, which pawed the ground, snorted and got a wild look
in its eye when anyone but Patrick mounted it.

Patrick had come off four miles back when the mare
slipped on a rocky incline, and plunged in an attempt to
recover its footing. Patrick, with the coffin across the
saddle in front, loosened his hold and the mare threw
him when a sharp corner dug into its shoulder. The mare
scrambled up the slope a few dozen yards on, but stopped, trembling and ashamed, when Patrick cried out, in
pain as it happened for he had broken a leg.

Leo turned his horse around, a rough bred pony the
McGoverns called Donkey, and slid off over Donkey's
obligingly lowered head. He went to Patrick grimacing

on the ground, grunting in his agony both with the leg and the sharp rocks on which he lay. "Gee Dad!" Leo cried, white of face. Patrick saw and lost some of his pain.

"Take the mare," said Patrick, and flung out an arm to ward off Leo, who was hovering above his injured leg, the snapped bone making a miniature tent of his trousers over the shin.

"The mare'll be faster," Patrick said, shutting his eyes. Leo held a branch of the wattle to help him stand without slipping. The mare curved its rubbery neck and snorted against its magnificent chest and Leo tried to meet its eye to plead tolerance.

"The box isn't damaged?" Patrick asked. He breathed in a way that alarmed Leo, but it was a way of controlling the pain, as he had showed Sarah when the births were imminent and the bush nurse not arrived.

Leo picked up the coffin and ran his hands and eyes around the edges. There was a slight splintering on one corner, and Leo stopped his hand on it and kept it there, although Patrick had his eyes closed and was grunting again.

"I steered it into the wattle when I was goin' down," Patrick said.

"It's not got a scratch Dad," Leo said, holding it gently as if it were a body.

"Just go and be careful," Patrick said. "Don't let on about me."

Now, several of the Coadys teetered on the edge of the veranda, wanting to rush to Leo but aware that this was not the time for normal behaviour. Mrs Coady took hold of the back of the rocking chair, and the oldest

Coady girl of about eighteen turned and put her face on her mother's neck and wept, and another much younger, frightened by this, burst into tears too. The mother, whose skirt was long and full, bunched a handful and put it against the child's face. She sniffed into it briefly then let it fall away and turned her head, eyes dry and clear, to watch Leo lay the coffin on the veranda edge.

"Dad didn't come," he said. "Only me." He turned the back of his neck to the Coadys to look at the way he had come, checking foolishly that there was no evidence of Patrick, whom he saw swiftly in his mind's eye, sweating with his tightly shut eyes and nowhere else for his elbows but the sharp stones. Now he was relieved of the coffin he would ride back in good time, then on to get Kevin and Lennie to carry Patrick home on the stretcher they would make from corn bags and two poles.

His hands itched for it and he nearly ran to the mare, ashamed he was not offering sympathy to the Coadys, knowing there was something he should say, remembering his mother's death and the callers wringing his father's hand and saying things with eyes lowered, and patting the heads of the younger McGoverns. Leo could not see himself patting Coady heads, except he would not have minded a hand among the thick fair curls of a girl named Rose who was aged about twelve and who had left the group to put her back to a veranda post, perhaps asking for attention in this way.

Leo tied the mare to a tree at the top of the ridge, it with a wild eye towards Patrick and Leo, scrambling down feeling wonderfully free without the coffin as if both his arms had been returned to him.

Patrick moved and grimaced. "Keep ridin'. And bring back a stretcher and Kevin and Lennie."

Leo wanted to say he'd thought of this as he started to scramble up the slope. He turned once to look at Patrick, who despite the pain in his eyes was checking the mare for damage just as he had checked the coffin.

Leo, with a sudden urge to show off, sent the mare flying across the ridge and down a slope, throwing his own body sideways as it swung around a thicket of saplings and galloped in the luxury of a clearing, hoping Patrick could hear the ring of hoofs, glad he was well clear of a reprimand.

Nearing home he galloped the mare again and it brought several McGoverns out, the white of Mrs McGovern's apron like a flag raised to herald the return. She hurried back inside and Leo thought she would be seeing to the kettle, more concerned with that than the absence of Patrick. But as Leo came closer he could sense their anxiety at seeing him on the mare, with no Patrick or Donkey, and he galloped harder to warn them to prepare for bad news.

"Some empty corn bags from the shed!" he called, flinging himself off the mare and tying it to the clothesline post. He pulled the props from the line, sending it dancing about, and called "Steady there!" when the mare danced too.

"Dad's broke his leg," he said, and laying the props by the veranda, pulled his hat off and put it on again. Mrs McGovern came from the kitchen with a pushed forward pinched face and Frances handed the baby to ten-year-old Irene who received it with joy, as an honour denied her up till now. She rewrapped the infant in its blanket, clearing its face of the cloth as she had seen her elders do, her small face changing, creasing with an adult concern and tenderness.

Frances ran towards the barn and Mrs McGovern brought a mug of water for Leo, and while he drank it buttered some damper and made the slices into a paper parcel. Mr McGovern brought a bottle one quarter full of brandy, holding it up to the sun and squinting at it. "Fetch a shoulder bag someone!"

Leo rode and Kevin and Lennie walked with the props and the bags. Kevin thought he should be riding the mare, since he was the eldest.

"Make sure you know the way!" he shouted.

For answer Leo raced the mare into a thicket shutting it from view, grinning at the "Hey there!" Kevin shouted.

Leo trotted the mare back into sight, jumping a log. "We should take turns!" Kevin cried, running and panting.

Leo put a protective hand on the bag, steadying the sloshing of the brandy bottle. He took it out and squinted at it as his grandfather had done.

"You dare drink that!" Kevin called, and Lennie dropped his prop with a bag wrapped around it.

"We'll pull him off and punch him!" Kevin yelled. The mare plunged at this and whinnied, and Leo like a seasoned horseman settled himself in the saddle, squaring his shoulders and giving the mare a pat on its quivering neck.

Kevin and Lennie used the props to thrash at some reeds bordering a swamp they were about to cross. Leo dug a dry boot into the mare's side and it went nimble-footed through the slush and up the bank.

"We'll kill the mongrel!" Kevin cried, wrenching the prop from the bog. He pointed it at Leo as if it were a spear he was about to throw.

Leo patted the mare again to settle it. He took out the brandy bottle and spread his hand in a show of unscrew-

ing the cap. He put back his head and raised the bottle
to his lips.

"He's not drinking it!" Kevin cried.

"He's not either!" Lennie echoed.

The mare twisted its rump in mild agitation and Leo
put the bottle back in the bag.

"See, he didn't screw no cap back on!" Kevin said.

Leo raised himself upright in the stirrups. "Weeeee,
yew-w-w-w, ahhhhh, wheeeee!" he yelled, taking off his
hat and twirling it above his head.

"The mongrel's not drunk!" panted Kevin.

He waved the prop and the bag slid off and he caught
it up and flung it over a shoulder, where it prickled him
cruelly through his sweat-soaked shirt. "The mongrel
bastard!" he whimpered.

Leo swung the mare towards the mountain. "Yew-w,
oooop!" he called, and Kevin and Lennie had to stop
and listen for the direction of the galloping hooves.

"If we lose the way we're done for," Lennie whined.

"The cunning bastard'll make sure he leaves tracks!"
Kevin cried.

A mile on, looking down from an outcrop of rocks,
they saw Leo's old striped cambric shirt billowing like a
sail from the top of a wattle.

"The bloody show-off!" Kevin said, mostly with
relief.

"Cooo-eee!" Lennie yelled, before Kevin could stop
him.

"You fool! Let him think we're not comin'!"

But Donkey whinnied in reply and the shirt was given
new life, jumping about when Leo scaled the tree and
thrashed at the branch.

*   *   *

Patrick was very pale, hadn't moved his leg and had wet his trousers.

"Look at that," he said, nodding with shamed shut eyes at the dark stain on his dungarees.

"Take a swig of this," Leo replied, taking the brandy bottle from the bag.

Patrick left his hand lying lightly on his chest. It seemed such a frail hand all of a sudden, as if it were someone else's. Leo laid the bottle on the grass and looked at his own hands joined between his knees and couldn't understand why his eyes began to fill with tears. He stood to his full height and squinted down on the thicket of trees spread on the next slope.

"Slow bastards," he mumured.

Kevin was allowed to swear, Lennie had tried it once and been whipped. Leo looked down with surprise on the immobility of Patrick, more surprised at the jerk of his mouth into a little smile.

"I didn't know before how tall you was," Patrick said.

A Stupid Child

Jane Hickson sat on Jonathon's knee at the Bennetts' party in front of everyone about an hour after they had eaten.

Jonathon Bennett and his wife Susan had given the party mainly because Jonathon had wanted to. In the past year the four couples, the Bennetts, the Hicksons, Jane and Mark, Lloyd and Freda Tait and the Penningtons, Tony and Ros, had been entertained at the other three homes. Jonathon said it was their turn and when Susan sent fine lines flying into her forehead and her eyes became a sharper blue, Jonathon said they could get cooked seafood from the new place in Lindfield, where for quite a reasonable outlay you got a large platter of mixed seafood, squid and prawns and scallops included.

"What outlay?" Susan asked. She was very careful with the money. He said he thought forty dollars, although he knew it was nearer to fifty, and then she asked if there would be enough for the children as well. The four couples had seven between them.

"Make sandwiches for the kids," Jonathon said.

He was tall and fair. He and Susan had almost iden-

tical colouring. They were often said to look alike, a few
light freckles on their skins, their hair curling at temples
and ears. When it was damp with perspiration, for they
worked in the garden a lot, it was exactly the same.

Once their elder child Celia had taken a handful of
strands from each head when they were sitting close
together, looking with pleasure on the pile of weeds they
had removed from the base of the grapefruit tree. Celia
crossed the hair from one head to the other.

"It is the same!" she cried and called for her little sister
Loris to come and look.

"Go and get our hats," Susan had said and Celia ran
into the house with her loping gait, her rump poked out,
her skirt swishing from side to side in a way that made
them laugh, although Celia would have locked herself in
her room and sobbed on her bed if she had known.

She bought the hats, a pink towelling one for her
mother and one the same for Jonathon in blue, bought
as a sort of joke when they were seventeen and started
going out together and their friends said they had to
have some way of telling them apart. They put them on
and remembering she smiled and rubbed her chin on her
raised knee, and he blushed and his eyes watered as they
had done when the two of them paired off at high
school, and were the only ones not to swim naked during a class picnic at Wiseman's Ferry, but went into the
bush instead, and sheltering under a rock, took their
clothes off for each other.

They were not ones to embrace in public. Celia,
because she saw her friends' parents kissing and fondling
each other, not minding who was around, was disappointed at this. Once, she had joined their hands when
the four of them were out walking, holding them
together for half a minute as if she had used glue and
needed to wait for it to dry. But the hands soon fell

apart, his to point out a kookaburra to Loris and hers to fall on Celia's shoulder.

When Jane, who was slightly overweight, suddenly plopped down on Jonathon's knee, he jerked upwards in surprise and went very pink and caused Jane's drink to splash on her thigh, covered in the blue silk fabric of her harem style trouser suit. He brushed at the splash and she brushed too, laughing. He trailed his hand away slowly, allowing his finger tips to rest, dug in ever so slightly, in the crease separating Jane's stomach and thigh.

Celia fastened her eyes there.

"Outside, Celia!" Susan said. "Watch that Loris doesn't climb to the top of the treehouse!"

This made Celia swoop around and run, for she kept forgetting the treehouse, Jonathon having finished it only that morning in time for the party. She gave a last blue look to Jonathon's hand still there, dimpling the stuff of Jane's trousers. Then she looked over her shoulder at Susan, asking with her eyes that Susan do something about the hand while she was gone.

Jonathon called Susan "darl" most of the time and she called him "honey". When the visitors had left and it was close to dinner time, he being the better cook of the two made a sauce for the remaining seafood. The dish came from the oven spitting yellow saliva, little peaks rising and curling their brown tops like tiny springs.

"That looks great, honey!" Susan cried, and Celia stuck out the little finger of her right hand under cover of the tablecloth.

She would count the number of times Susan and Jonathon used their terms of endearment for each other, using a hand for each.

Jonathon frowned from the opposite side of the table at the awkward use of her fork with a finger separated from the others. She curled it, hoping it would be less obvious, and since she was constantly berated for her finicky eating habits she made a sudden energetic stab at a thick flake of cheese and took it between her teeth, keeping her lips free of it, which was her way of treating most foods.

"She's a hopeless eater!" Jonathon said, and did not flash accusing eyes at Susan, although Celia felt by fixing his eyes on his plate he actually was.

"I gave them their sandwiches later than I should have," Susan said, and Celia thought by the way she looked down she didn't want to eat any more either.

Jonathon got up and took some empty dishes to the sink, and then ran out and down the back steps so fast it seemed the screen door had barely slammed shut before he'd driven the spade into a garden bed so deeply he had to waggle the handle several times to get it out.

"Don't you want coffee, honey?" Susan called from the kitchen window.

Celia dropped her fork and put her second finger against the little one. Outside, the spade made urgent thudding noises and Celia listened for it to trail off into a slower, more dreamy rhythm; but it didn't, and she marvelled at her father's energy sustained for so long. Perhaps it worried Susan too, there with her hands resting on the sink and her mouth like a small wrinkled questioning strawberry.

Celia still had her left hand with all the fingers together. She felt sad and silly looking at it, and decided to put it to better use by sliding a good portion of her meal onto Loris's plate, Loris being of sturdy frame with an appetite to match. Loris began to squeak a protest, then caught sight of a fat prawn and picked it from the sauce in triumph, wishing the Pennington boy could see, his passion for prawns having been disclosed to her in a whine while they ate cheese and celery sandwiches under the liquidambar, with crusts dropped on them by the older ones in the treehouse.

Susan put her daughters to bed and read them a story while Jonathon dug on, the twilight seeming to soften the sound. Loris raised herself to see, through the window, his head ducking above the spade which squeaked between the thuds as if protesting against overuse.

"Daddy is digging and digging and *digging*," she said, lying flat again.

The girl's name in the story was Jane. She had a sister Susan. "Jane and Susan!" said Loris.

"All stories have those names," Celia said, and the last sentence Susan had read hung for a moment in the air between the beds.

Loris shook her knee. "Go *on*," she said.

Celia turned her face to the wall, "I can listen with my back."

Celia and Jane's daughter Emily were in the same class at school. Emily's house was in the street that crossed the end of Celia's street. It was Celia's habit to wait at her gate and, when Emily turned the corner, cross to the footpath opposite, and the two would walk the three blocks to the school. Some mornings Jane walked with them as far as the village centre where she had a partnership with a cousin in a business, Cutmore Cakes. The two women did most of their own baking, building up a reputation for their cheese cakes, tortes, eclairs and brandy snaps, and lately Jane's cheese and herb scones. Although the shop did not open until ten o'clock, Jane went early on the busier days, of which Monday was one, for an extra hour in the shop kitchen.

Celia was startled to see Jane with Emily this Monday morning.

She went hot all over as she did when she discovered

the simplest things had been overlooked. She then thought she really was stupid as a lot of people said.

"Stupid!" her father said when she splashed wildly at a swimming lesson, fearful of drowning, believing she would sink during the time her arm was raised out of the water, if she dared stop for a moment her frantic threshing.

"Not Celia Bennett!" Frances Fielding, captain of the netball team, would implore the school sports mistress. "She doesn't do *anything*!"

Here was Jane Hickson loaded with a great straw basket filled with flowers from her garden for the shop, and Emily running alongside with a bunch in the crook of her arm for their class teacher Mrs Land, swinging her schoolcase from one hand to the other for relief from its weight.

She would have to offer to carry something, Celia decided, not wanting to but running forward to take from Jane's plaited fingers a carry bag of baking pans, borrowed from the shop kitchen to make her herb bread. Jane was experimenting with great enthusiasm with her home-grown herbs, and the herb bread had been her contribution to the Bennetts' luncheon.

Celia saw the tin and remembered.

Jonathon had gone very pink when he saw the bread and wrapped his arms around the tin which was still warm. His eyes had watered as they did when he was happy, and Celia had worried that he might cry.

He cried "Look, darl!" and Susan put her chin over his shoulder to breathe the fragrance of thyme and rosemary under the snowy cloth flung back.

She was terribly pleased because she had been worried that in keeping costs down she might have skimped on the menu. She flung her arms wide and embraced Jane and there they were, the dark, glossy, cropped head of

Jane and the fair one of Susan pressed together, and Celia, watching her mother and her best friend's mother in each other's arms and the two fathers standing off half shy about it but pleased too.

She felt as she had felt early one summer morning on holidays when Jonathon had taken her to watch the sun rise over the sea. It came up all on fire shooting out scarlet and purple arms and drawing them in just as quickly, shaking with its brightness, growing even brighter as she watched until she was afraid it might explode and shatter into a million pieces and drop into the sea.

If this happened the whole world would be plunged into darkness.

Jonathon told her not to be stupid, it would never happen that way.

Home Sick

The mother was young and pretty and not pleased and the small boy Edwin puny for his age and not pleased either, but for a different reason.

His was guilt.

He was home from school sick and it upset some plans of his mother's, he was sure of that. Their place was very small. He had no room of his own, so the couch where he slept at night was also his bed for convalescing in the daytime.

He had been sick yesterday too, one of the days his mother went to work folding tee-shirts in a factory. She was a tall blond woman with a lot of hair which she dressed in the old fashioned way piled on top of her head. Strands sprang out from the knot which always looked like slipping and coming loose, but seldom did.

When she was on her chair her head made a great shadow on the wall. He amused himself watching the shadow sometimes running into the corner and becoming nothing like her, the nose on both walls and the loose hair waving about like a hand directing traffic.

She did not sit down today, she was too restless and the lamp which made the shadows was not turned on anyway. It seemed she was keeping the room gloomy to match her mood.

He wished it was yesterday. He had had a better time, then, though he was sicker, with Mrs Grace coming in and out from her flat at the other end of the building, by arrangement with his mother.

Edwin had played a guessing game, listening for her footsteps, picking them out from others, from Mrs Tradowski's mostly, who was the same age and size as Mrs Grace, but a foreigner, so you would expect her steps to sound different. And they did, whispering on the wood, as if they were afraid it would shout harsh words back at her.

Mrs Grace rushed and slithered. It seemed she would slither past the door, but his fear turned immediately to delight, for there was a little silence before the doorknob turned. She had told his mother she would come in six times, three in the morning and three in the afternoon. He felt a rush of love at the way she kept her promise. He decided now he should cough from time to time to reassure his mother of his legitimate cause for staying at home again today. He coughed with effort for he was getting better. His mother's frown, turned on him from the sink, said he was feigning the cough.

The kitchen of their little flat was through an archway from the living room. There was a small bathroom at the end of the hall, only the width of the hall, and off the one bedroom a dusty little veranda with a canvas blind split in several places and a chair with bursting upholstery and the once toffee-coloured wood bleached to the colour of dirty sand.

Edwin had never been on the veranda and seldom in his mother's room, kept neat with the bed made and a rose coloured eiderdown folded at the foot, under which he would love to snuggle. Since the whole flat was dark her lamp with the rose coloured shade was on a lot of the time. When she did not quite close the door he glimpsed her in her white nightgown in bed in a pool of light, a rosy glow on her hair still with its know but very loose, her forehead whiter than in the daytime and her hands with the freckles gone. Her gold ring with the blue stones sharp enough to cut you was so alive it seemed about to leap from her finger.

Now at the sink she took the ring from the window sill where it rested while she washed her coffee cup and his milk mug. Her hands went spidery pushing the tea towel into his mug to dry it. She crossed her eyes on it, making her eyebrows spidery too. He must have done something wrong while drinking from it, although it was hard to think what.

She had not dressed so far, but was in her gown, the blue wool one with the satin binding on the lapels and the same binding edging the belt looped neatly on her flat stomach.

He closed his eyes in his little white face and decided he would play a game of guessing what she was doing. In a moment there was a tiny scratching noise, she was filing one of her nails, that would be right. Scratch, scratch, like a mouse with a crust of bread. Perhaps it was a mouse, somewhere near his feet, with some crumbs from his breakfast toast. The scratching was getting louder and braver. A mouse, for sure a mouse! He squeaked like one and flung up a foot under his blanket. She gave a startled sigh and dropped her arms against her gown. He saw she *had* been filing her nails and wished he could tell her how he had been right in the first place. He did not think she would be interested, looking at him in her cross-eyed way with her lips tight and stretched, digging right into her face without smiling. The face said it was his fault for stopping her from doing whatever it was she wanted to do.

If he could say "What do you want to do? Don't let me stop you," it would be wonderful. He read a lot and people in the stories spoke that way. But he felt encouraged to say something.

"Put on your blue dress, why don't you?" It was silky and loose and flopping at the top and tight and closely pleated at the bottom.

It did not hang on her like a dead thing, the way dresses did on mothers who came to his school (she never did) but tumbled and swirled and danced about as if her body gave it life.

For answer she blew hard on a nail, a kind of snorting blow like saying don't be stupid. Then she went on swift feet to the bedroom and closed the door. The telephone was there. He heard the little whirr of numbers dialled. He counted them. Six. Sometimes there were seven. It made no difference though. He didn't know who was at the end of any of them.

"Sometimes I think I do," he whispered, his eyes creeping to the door like furtive feet. He heard her murmuring voice but was unable to distinguish a word. Not one word.

"I might be deaf," he said quite loud to test his hearing.

"What?" She put her face in a crack of the door, the phone in her hand. "Thank you for your call, Mr Brown," said her haughty voice returned to the mouthpiece. When she had put the phone down she flung the door right back and asked with her spidery eyebrows what he wanted. He needed to think of something quick. He couldn't worry her with his deafness. He always heard best when he looked straight at mouths, so in future he would make sure he did. The ache down the side of his face was probably the reason why he wasn't hearing well, if he wasn't, but most likely he was anyway. She kept her voice low perhaps because of Mrs Grace who sometimes came in without knocking, saying she was worried that Edwin might be by himself. His mother said Mrs Grace wanted to know the ins and outs of the magpie's arsehole and to tell her nothing.

Low voices were intended for not hearing, he supposed, otherwise why make them low? He swallowed to test his throat. Swallowed again for another test. There was only the smallest hurt. He felt his groin which had been wet with sweat yesterday and last night. Dry. He put one side of his face on the pillow, not eager for the coolness as before, and he put an arm out in front of him. He believed it had thickened up since yesterday. He flexed it. Yes, look at that wobbling flesh. It didn't seem as long as it was yesterday either.

Here was some good news for her. He wouldn't tell her right away, though. Not immediately. It would be good to see her face while he said it. She was back at the sink looking over it through the window where there was only the wall of the flats next door to see. She had a hand on a hip, the fingers spread on the top of her rump.

"I'm better," he said loudly so that she could not fail to hear. His face felt very hot and he begged her in his thoughts not to keep staring at him. In the end she turned away to lift the kettle and shake it, checking if there was water there, then lighting the gas under it. Her blue sleeve shook as she waggled the match to put it out. Then she walked quickly back to her bedroom, shutting the door with a click, not an angry click, more of an uncertain one. He was still, thinking. Then he put his feet to the floor. The cold shot tiny pains up his legs. That's nothing much, he said to himself and lifted his school clothes from the chair where she had laid them the night before.

He had his shirt on, white and much too long for him, and one sock when the kettle boiled. The whistling always brought her running, angry that it was always she who had to see to it.

He turned the gas out and she was there beside him. He dodged around her gown to put on his other sock, and sat down because he was not too strong on his legs. She poured water into a mug on top of coffee grounds and put her back against the sink and her feet forward while she sipped, watching him finish dressing. It was terrible the way she did not speak. Here he was going all hot again stupidly.

"I'm going to school," he said.

She wrapped both hands around the mug and narrowed her eyes above the rim.

"You *are* better then," she said sounding as if there had been a long discussion about it. She rinsed the mug and set it to drain and suddenly in a great hurry went back to her room, frowning at the clock as she passed it.

He looked at it too. Right now at school Miss Hannaford would have the class singing the happy song. They sang it every morning in a big circle before they sat at their desks, standing in different places each time so they were next to different people. Or little people, as Miss Hannaford always said. After the song they shook the hand of the little person on the right, then on the left and asked if they were happy. And trotting back to their seats they sang Be happy, happy, happeee. All of us be happeee. It sounded terribly easy, except that Miss Hannaford expected everyone to look happy as well. She said if anyone was unhappy, he or she could be unhappy for the rest of the day.

He often thought she looked directly at him at this

point, making him think he might be the cause of all the unhappiness in the world. Many little people did look at him, right into his face, making it hard for him to work up a happy look.

But the happy song would be over by the time he got to the school and the class would be doing some real work.

Thank goodness. . .

Here Blue

The Tweedies had lived in Pine Valley all their lives. Old Mr and Mrs Tweedie were long since dead and buried on the slope at the northern end of the valley, in (naturally) a cemetery enclosed by pine trees.

There was a son Fergus, who like his sisters Caroline and Josephine had never married. Fergus had been an invalid since a stroke paralysed his left side in 1969. That was ten years ago and he had actually outlived old Doctor Newberry, who had told Caroline he would take another stroke and die. The only marked difference in Fergus since the ambulance had brought him from hospital in Newcastle thirty kilometres away was the increased whiteness of his hand, the right one which held his stick.

He never used the stick as it was intended, as Caroline on one side and Josephine on the other would take him from his bed to the veranda, and since he used bedpans, there was no necessity to take the brick and weed back path to the lavatory.

But he insisted on holding the stick, tangling it often in the legs of Josephine, whose legs were not unlike it, brown and long and skinny and hairless, never moving with grace, but rather as if her body was irritated by their failure to coordinate, and the legs in retaliation moved in spasms of snaps and jerks.

When Fergus was under his rug, he laid the stick sloping towards the floor, his fine old fingers holding it with a gentleness that was deceptive. His features settled into tranquillity, the hostility gone from his one good eye, the good side of his mouth no longer puckered, as if the journey from bed to veranda had been as challenging as one across an unfriendly desert, but he had made it in safety.

Caroline and Josephine had their own systems of recovery. Caroline used to slap to the kitchen in her big loose slippers and raise a big noise washing the breakfast things; Josephine, depending on the smoothness or otherwise of the journey with Fergus, would call Blue, the fat, spotted blue and white crossbred cattle dog, usually asleep in a corner of the yard like a mound of mouldy porridge.

This morning Josephine did not call Blue immediately, but sat on the top veranda step and turned a big fold of her skirt back to stroke her legs from the ankles up.

"Stop that," said Fergus, although his eyes were closed.

Josephine pressed her head down between her knees so far that only the top showed, her hair very wild, black and curly, swirling from her crown. She appeared to be staring into her fork.

"Stop that," said Fergus, his stick scraping the floor.

Josephine sprang up, quick and lithe as a boy, and caught the beam above her head. She swung out over the steps, her legs like two poles, thin ones, making her shoes seem large and loose.

"See the poppy show!" she called out. The postman passing their gate (there was never any mail for the

Tweedies) lowered his head until it just skimmed the handlebars of his bicycle.

"Linnie!" Fergus called. "See what she's doing!"

Josephine swung wide and clapped her shoes together. Caroline's feet clapped the floor on their way from the kitchen, and Josephine landed on the veranda as she reached it. They looked at each other with a dozen boards between them. Caroline was white of face with bluish lips, her eyes only a shade more blue, pink mottling on her large cheeks, whitish grey eyebrows and some more of the same hairs curling from a mole at the corner of her mouth, a few more strewn across her upper lip. Josephine had a long brown face with a long sharp nose and a small mouth, made smaller by biting at her lip, as if she intended to remove it altogether. The two faces met now like two flags, one strong-coloured, pretty sure of victory, the other preparing to be lowered in defeat.

"Blue! Here, Blue!" Josephine called, not taking her eyes from Caroline's face, her own darkening with blood at the strain of yelling. Fergus jabbed the floor with his stick and Blue, yelping and growling, hurled himself through the back doorway, skittered down the hall on the linoleum, landed at the feet of Josephine, and scrambled to his own, throwing them onto Josephine's skirt, his slobbering and snuffling face on her thigh.

Caroline took Blue's head and swung it away very hard and he went ambling with lowered head down the steps, his tail beating on his anus as if that was guilty too.

Josephine slapped her thigh and went through the gate. Mrs Looney in the house next door came to the front with her broom, leaning so hard on it the straws were squashed halfway up. To straighten them Mrs Looney slapped the broom head against a veranda post.

"Good morning Mrs Looney!" called Josephine, holding Blue back by grabbing a piece of skin on his neck.

"Gooday Josie." Mrs Looney swiped at cobwebs on the timber trimming above her head. She wanted to know about the yelling but didn't want any truck with Josephine. "Fergus well?"

Blue gave a frantic bark and looked back at the Tweedies' place. Josephine sank down on the grass and wrapped an arm around his body. He raised himself on his hind legs, his paws on Josephine's shoulders, his behind quivering, his eyes quite wild.

"A disgusting sight!" said Mrs Looney, but no one heard. She gave a cobweb a last slap and went inside.

"We'll run, boy, we'll run!" Josephine cried, and did.

A little way along was the Cannons' house, the bouncing clothesline indicating Mrs Cannon pegging out clothes. She was very young, only twenty, with a baby yelling inside the house.

The way the line jigged about told of her hurry to get in and see to it. Josephine took a handful of Blue's neck to stop him charging off, while she waited for Mrs Cannon, who was Isabel Grant before her marriage, to reach the end of the line, no longer hidden by the house.

"Hello Iss!" Josephine called.

Mrs Cannon waved and dashed up her back steps. The baby's crying worried and irritated her, her husband Milton might be home early if there was a miners' strike, as he had said there would be, and she would have nothing done. If Josie came in she supposed she could hand her the baby to hold while she washed the breakfast things. She tiptoed with the quietened baby on her shoulder and peered between the slit in the curtains of the front room. Josie was rubbing her shoe on Blue's belly. His paws and crooked back legs were in the air and his back was writhing in the dead burrs and dust of the Cannons' nature strip.

"Milt would kill me if I let her touch the baby," Mrs Cannon said, sneaking to the kitchen.

"We won't see the ickle baby," Josie was saying sadly to Blue. Then she bounded ahead and he raced and sprawled on the gravel road in his hurry, and came back to yap wildly at her feet.

Pine Valley village was a few hundred yards down the dip. There was not much life there since two mines had closed down in the seventies. The cooperative store was reduced to half its former size, the other half converted to living quarters where the present owner Mrs Molly Crapp lived alone.

When it became the first cash and carry store for Pine Valley it was well patronised by locals, who felt a little of the big city of Newcastle had overflowed along the cracked bitumen road to them. Shopping would be cheaper with no grocer boy to pay, the old counters and bins of flour, sugar and rice gone, everything in packets and tins for self service.

But the roads were sealed to make them fit for the cars that everyone needed, to get them to work in the city, and this was where most people bought their food supplies. The last owner before Mrs Crapp left when his daughter refused to give up her leisure time after school to man the checkout. To improve her case for leaving Pine Valley, she cunningly formed an association with a widower who had two children and did occasional carrying jobs to augment his miner's pension. The father quarrelled with the carrier, saw his stock dwindle away, got a job as a storeman in a Newcastle store and took his family there, selling out to Mrs Crapp who had a widow's pension and a casual attitude towards the business. She opened and closed at her own convenience, and did not stock any new lines. Her refrigerator leaked in the summer and iced up so badly in winter that children brought in small toys and played with them on imaginary snow covered mountains.

Mrs Crapp had lank grey hair bobbed just clear of her shoulders, a reddish tan face with black eyebrows, and brown eyes, round and dull. They did not change expression even when the rest of her face softened with pleasure, rare though these occasions were. Mrs Crapp drank, slipping through the partition to her rooms several times a day. She couldn't go to sleep without her snort and often failed to wake up because of it, aroused eventually by children banging on the shop door, sent by their mothers for butter or canned sandwich fillings, too afraid to return home without the items, aware they could be sent to school without lunch if they did.

Mrs Crapp had the shop open when Josephine and Blue looked in. She was by the till picking through some apples and tomatoes in the bottom of a crate. She rubbed an apple on her breast and bit into it. Josephine came in with Blue at her heels and took an apple too. There was a rotten spot on it. She bit this out and spat it across the floor. Blue ran his chin over it, snorted, then lay down and stared at it.

Mrs Crapp, noting that Josephine appeared to have no money on her, gave the apple piece a curt kick through the door. It hit the knee of Mr Andy Walters, editor of the *Pine Valley News*, who was on his way in. Josephine laughed and banged her half eaten apple on her thigh for she was balanced against the turnstile, there being no chairs in the shop since the days of the long counter and storage bins. Mrs Crapp tipped the apples and tomatoes into the window, disturbing a contingent of flies, tiny black ones that made the bananas even blacker.

"Shoo!" She slapped a hand among them, and when she turned and straightened up with help from a thrown back chin and a hand rubbing at the small of her back, the flies spread themselves among the apples and raced with joy into some holes in the tomatoes.

"No ads from me Andy!" she said, flinging the crate against the wall. "I made seventy-five cents for meself last week!"

"I'm full up Molly," Andy said. This was one time Molly allowed herself a little smile.

Andy had had a good bi-weekly newspaper once, and a reporter helping him. Now it was a monthly double sheet which he wrote and laid out and sent to printers in Newcastle. He distributed it himself from his old car. At some Pine Valley houses the last two or three issues would be lying sodden and discoloured in gutters and long grass. The columns had less and less advertising in them and more and more of Andy's two line pleas to shop locally and support the local paper.

"Ah, it's not like the old days, is it?" Molly said, opening the till and slamming it shut after checking its empty state.

"It sure isn't," Andy said, turning sideways on the ledge and drawing his big legs up. "Throw us a pack of fags, Moll."

Molly took a pack of cigarettes from a shelf above the till and tossed them to Andy. She caught up a pencil on a string bound to a nail driven into the shelf and entered the purchase in a notebook.

"I won't forget," Andy said with irritation.

"A lot do," Molly said. She ruffled the pages as if to say there was all the evidence required. "In the old days it didn't matter. There were enough good payers to pay for the bad ones."

"We're good payers," Josephine said, folding her arms across her chest.

Blue twitched a nose, dark grey and wrinkled like a lizard's back. He growled low in agreement.

"I said that mongrel shouldn't be in here," Molly said, putting a rusted tin of soup someone had returned on the notebook to flatten a dog-eared corner.

"Outside, hound!" cried Andy. He wanted to take home a can of beans for his lunch, needing credit for this as well as the cigarettes, so he felt obliged to side with Molly.

"How's Tilly?" Molly asked, sharpening the pencil with big, outward strokes of a knife she used for cutting pumpkin.

"Pains everywhere as usual." Andy flicked ash from his cigarette on the floor, then rubbed a toe of his shoe into it. Blue got up and ran a sniff expertly around the shoe.

"That mongrel's starved!" Molly cried. "Take him home and feed him!"

"Fergus gets pains," Josephine said. "A lot."

Molly went to the back of the shop, returning with a mop and bucket, for it was summer and the refrigerator had spread a pool of water on the floor.

"Fetch me a can of beans on your way back!" Andy called.

Molly wrung out the grey-white mop with grey-brown hands and shook it. "I'm makin' a fortune today alright!" She dropped the bucket partly out of sight behind the refrigerator, and returning to the front stopped and went back to take a can of beans from a shelf, rubbing an end down her side to remove some dust.

She threw it to Andy who caught it and balanced it on a knee, closing an eye on it as if it were a target for a shooting exercise. Blue leapt up to stand on his hind legs and bark at the tin, his tool showing a tip of red quivering towards it. Molly opened her mouth then closed it. She took the pencil and pushed it between her lips, opened the notebook, seemed to be searching for a page, then returned her gaze to Blue, his belly on the floor again. Molly lifted her chin sharply and Blue rose again, the red point darting out and quivering back.

Andy dropped his big feet to the floor. Molly put the book back under the tin and opened the lid of another, a larger one on the floor near her feet. She pawed through the broken biscuits half filling it, and going to Blue held two up. Blue rose high, pawing the air, the pale spots on his pink belly shaking. She dropped the biscuits into his mouth one at a time. He swallowed them in snaps then rose for more. Molly put the toe of her shoe on his belly to turn his head towards the door. She went ahead of him and he followed, running his lizardly nose up to and around her skirt hem.

"Out!" she cried, pointing to the step. Blue ambled across it and onto the ground and Josephine joined him with the same ambling gait.

Molly watched them bob down the road, the hot midday sun shrinking them and outlining their shapes with a great gold pen.

"They're gone," she called out, addressing the back of the shop.

For a while Pine Valley village was empty of people, then Mrs Annie Mannix appeared and so did young Peter Canning. Mrs Mannix wanted rice for a pudding and young Canning wanted to sell his bicycle and put the money towards a motor bike which would get him to Newcastle to look for work. He had the For Sale advertisement written out by his mother in his hand on the bicycle handlebar.

When they saw Mrs Crapp's shop and Andy's newspaper office both with their doors shut, one said to the other that Pine Valley was surely going to the dogs.

Whatever Pa Says

Henry Crowley built a nice brick home in the hamlet of Hoxton in northern New South Wales and worked his property two miles away.

Some time later he acquired more land, part of a mountain peak, and after clearing it single-handed grew bananas, transforming the lantana-infested and rocky terrain to a proud maiden with a slender neck rising from a gown of layered green silk.

Henry had no sons to help him, but he never complained, going off mostly at daybreak in his old truck to tend his pineapples on the flat and his bananas on the hills.

His wife Mildred and the girls, Anastacia, Monica and Julia seldom went near the place.

At fifteen Julia did.

There was a galvanised iron shed opening onto the main road where Henry stored his tractor and packing cases for his fruit, some rough benches in a corner and a tap coming through from a tank outside. Henry filled a chaff bag with straw and flung it down for a bed, when he needed to pack bananas far into the night, or the creek was up too high to cross in the truck. At such times he always reminded Mildred that he'd never failed to get through with the horse and sulky, although he was forward-thinking enough to cultivate a crop of avocado trees, which the other farmers said was a waste of effort, since the fruit tasted and looked like green axle grease and he had no hope of marketing it.

Julia visited the farm when a skinny, but muscular part-Aboriginal boy called Alex Crowe (black as a crow the locals said, but he wasn't, just milk chocolate coloured with pink palms and pale blue nails and better teeth than most of them) was employed by Henry to help out over a busy period. Henry kept finding more for him to do. He seemed satisfied with a few shillings a week in pay, and Henry brought a discarded food safe from the house where he could store his bread and cans of camp pie and bottle of tomato sauce, and after a few weeks a jar of Mildred's plum jam, green tomato relish and a large portion of newly baked currant loaf carried under Julia's coat. Mildred and the other girls, too late, would see Julia flying past the neighbours' houses with an orchard and a corn paddock separating each from the other and about to take the turn towards the Crowley farm.

"Don't sing out!" Mildred would urge them, before Stacia and Monnie could get their mouths open. Greater was her shame at neighbours suspecting disharmony in the Crowley household than shame at any hint of its cause.

This came later when Alex and Julia made good use of the hay bed while Henry sweated among the bananas, his old boots sturdily gripping the sloping ground, the trees' green banners stroking his blue singlet back. If he had been a man of humour he would have laughed at the sly way the fruit hid as if it wanted to keep to itself the progress of its growth and surprise him one day when it was ripe for picking, no longer tiny green hunchbacked grubs clinging to a mother's nourishing back.

Julia had just turned sixteen when she found she was pregnant and there was a terrible row in the kitchen, Mildred running to shut all the windows, distraught with the noise and cursing to herself the day she agreed to Henry giving the house four bedrooms when the girls could have shared one. Then Julia could not so easily have sneaked out at midnight to meet Alex and make love in the orchard with ripe plums plopping down around them. (Julia confessed to this but remained silent about the hay bed mainly to protect Alex, since Henry's wrath would have been fuelled to explosion point had he known he was paying for time spent in broad daylight tumbling with his daughter).

As it was, his rage set him pacing the kitchen and he kicked out at Alex on a chair, Alex immediately standing, appearing to unfold himself into a greater height, so that Julia standing too lifted her chin to look into his face, puzzled somewhat because normally she was as tall as he. His mouth worked but he did not get any words out, looking down on his grimy old tweed cap trailing on a thigh. Julia seemed silently urging him to speak, whatever it was he said she would totally support. Stacia had the irrational thought that he was superior in his colour. His skin was like the crust of a newly baked loaf. Henry was pale like an uncooked loaf. Mildred and Monnie and herself too, she suspected, were like the cowering unbaked loaves lined up on the kitchen table to go in the oven when there was space, anxious that they should come out well, afraid they might not.

Alex and Julia left the kitchen with no one following them and Julia crying softly while she filled a straw basket with some clothes from her room. Alex waited at the top of the veranda steps, too afraid to glance backwards, believing the windows were more Crowley eyes watching him, and when she came on her gentle feet around the corner, he took the basket under one arm and used the other to take her hand, and they set out to walk to Lismore.

He had some money and so did she. They caught a train to Grafton, and started from there on a long walk into higher timbered country, where there was a station settled by a rich German, who had his house built as a replica of a castle on the Rhine. He employed blacks as stockmen and rouseabouts, and white girls were in demand to work in the house, but few stayed because of the isolation. Julia was given a job as housemaid, being quick and bright and no longer pregnant.

She had miscarried ten miles along the road from Grafton, and a buggy flagged down by Alex had taken her to a cottage hospital where she passed, in a river of blood and with an agonising thirst, something that looked like a potato sprouting four little stunted shoots. She was ready next day to continue the walk, Alex having slept overnight in the back of a buggy in the hospital shed. Luckily it was a mild March and he was warm enough with a corn bag covering him and some of Julia's clothes taken from the basket for a pillow.

They did not get married since there was no child to worry about, and soon became absorbed in separate cultures, Alex becoming a stockman and fine horseman, given to understand the homestead was out of bounds to him, while Julia, a favourite of her mistress, became devoted to the child born a few months after she and Alex arrived. She saw in the baby the image of the one she had lost. When the child Elsa was a toddler Julia went with the family to Germany for a three months' visit. In her absence Alex went to Queensland, lured there by reported opportunities to take out big prize money in rodeo events, his passion for riding taking precedence over what remnants were left of his passion for Julia.

Alex's departure was the only cheering feature of the return to Australia for Julia's mistress. No longer was there any threat of disruption to Julia's role as devoted servant and companion, except for a minor (and later acceptable) upheaval, when Elsa went to St Mary's Convent in Grafton as a boarder, and Julia, pining for her, followed and took a job as a general help in a doctor's home. She saw Elsa at every opportunity, visiting the convent and taking her out when she had leave at weekends and public holidays.

Nothing of this was known to Henry and Mildred, Stacia and Monnie. When Julia and Alex had passed through the village and along the road towards Lismore nearly ten years earlier, Henry had brought his fist down on the table with a terrible bang. He sat down then with his face white and stared at the place his fist had struck as if watching for a split or a hole. Mildred, because she did not know what else to do, put the kettle over the heat to make tea, although the fountain (built into the side of the stove and allowed to get low on water because of the row) was puffing steam from its brass mouth, blowing out a message that it was in urgent need of replenishing.

"The fountain, Ma," Stacia said, nodding at it. Henry's head shot up at the sound of her voice as if he had, in losing Julia, lost the rest of his family too. For the first time in the memory of any of them Henry got up and unhooked a cup from the dresser and looked at the big brown teapot as if through some miracle there was freshly brewed tea in it.

"Oh Pa!" said Mildred starting to cry.

They had all rushed then to make afternoon tea, the

three of them crying, Monnie slicing brown bread thinly as Henry liked it, and rubbing her eyes with her fist, the carving knife still in it, sawing menacingly at the air.

"Ain't there no handkerchiefs in the place?" Henry cried, and took his own, a folded checked one, and laid it on a knee. They did everything as usual, setting up the gate-legged table and spreading it with the spoke-stitched linen cloth, Stacia looking over it for anything missing, remembering the fig jam, Henry's favourite, and running to the pantry for it. Mildred, checking too, remembered the oatmeal biscuits she had made that morning, pleasure rushing to her face when she opened the tin and the smell rushed up at her, then leaving it just as quickly, crumpling it at the memory of Julia seizing one from the tray, holding it up and opening her mouth like a bird, allowing the hot pieces to plop into it.

They gathered around the table trying to make nothing of her empty place, Monnie straightening the chair that had always been hers, and Stacia fixing her watering eyes on it, the back so erect, making her think of a tombstone, and the white cloth empty in her place like a church altar, the sun sending sparks off the silver sugar bowl like a communion chalice. She half expected a priest's white hands with nails pale as celluloid spread around it to lift it with great tenderness and reverence and hold it above their bowed heads.

But it was Henry's brown hands with their brown scarred nails and flapping shirt sleeves that grasped the bowl, tipping it roughly towards him.

"Excuse me!" Stacia said, the words squeaking their way through her throat, and laying down the spoke-stitched napkin she fled to her room. Henry stirred his tea, looking over the heads of Mildred and Monnie at the window where Mildred's geraniums bloomed scarlet and purple and white in their pots on the sill, as if their beauty had captured his attention and he was partly reluctant to turn it elsewhere, a small resigned sigh accompanying the gesture of taking the last piece of bread and butter.

Mildred, with a throat too full for food, felt the shame of betrayal. I am not crying though, that is one good thing, and aloud she said: "Oooh, that tea's hot!" to account for her watering eyes.

Henry put on a khaki tunic, a relic of the Great War, and Mildred wanted to cry out that the day was too hot for it, then closed her hand over her mouth to hold back a cry of fear that he was leaving them forever as well. Stacia, who was back in the kitchen when she heard the truck start up, watched from the window until she saw it turn towards the farm, not towards Lismore as she half believed it might in pursuit of Julia.

She turned back to the table, worrying that she had no energy, no desire to clear it.

The inside of the cups were spattered with tea leaves, Monnie's cup nearly full of greying tea, a skin forming on the top. There was a trail of crumbs towards Henry's place, a sultana trapped in a spoke stitch. Monnie had grown terribly small on her chair. Mildred sat on hers against the wall. All of them thought the table would stay like that forever, the saucers ending up stuck to the cloth wearing circles through to the wood, the two slices of cake left overlapping each other, reduced first to crumbs then to fine dusty yellow powder, the cloth shredding until it too became part of the wood, everything a murky, ugly, greyish colour, the way they saw all their future.

"Whatever will we do?" asked the quaking voice of Monnie.

Whatever will *she* do? wondered Mildred, seeing Julia with her skin gone dark, her legs long and thin and her belly round and her hair black and matted, walking strung out across the road with others, carrying a sugar bag of fish or a bunch of bananas across a shoulder, her hooped back black with flies, turning around calling to straggling children. Her child? More children? A child in that round belly? The agony of childbirth under a tree, sweating and feebly brushing at flies, an old gin crouched over a fire, stirring ashes, the ashes to coat the newborn child because there were no clothes or shawl to wrap it in.

Mildred got up from her chair and Stacia and Monnie stood too, tilting their chins to search Mildred's face, as Julia had searched the face of Alex for direction.

"We'll do whatever Pa wants," Mildred said.

Julia's name was never mentioned in Henry's hearing. They talked about her when Henry was at the farm. Even then Mildred usually took up a position by the nearest window, looking out with an anxious face. It was not clear if she feared the unexpected appearance of Henry or was saddened anew at the thought of Henry's total rejection of his daughter.

Mildred took Stacia and Monnie to Brisbane for two weeks' holiday a few days after Julia left.

"It'll stop the talk," Mildred said.

"What talk?" asked Henry, with frightening calm in his eyes above the cigarette he was rolling.

In Brisbane they stayed where they usually did, close to the Botanic Gardens, and spent a lot of time walking there. Mildred bought new shoes for Stacia and Monnie which rubbed their heels, then blistered them, and they had to wear their old ones again, miserable with discomfort and disappointment, believing everyone was pitying their shabby footwear.

"It's her fault," Monnie said, perspiring with pain on a garden seat.

"I want to go home too," Stacia said, starting to remove the shoe from the foot with the worst blister, then baulking at the thought of the agony getting it on again.

Henry collected them at Lismore railway station. With a new car.

They were standing looking out for the truck, each of the girls hoping it would be the other who would sit on the back with the cases in full view of Hoxton, for there were sure to be people about and the tennis courts full on a Saturday afternoon.

But here was this shiny navy blue Essex with pale grey canvas blinds, a square of clear perspex in the middle, only big enough to show a face, and Henry coming from it not smiling, treating it as if it were still the old truck, then bending to pick up their cases, looking at none of them as was his way and walking quickly back to the new car.

"Oh, Pa," Mildred said in a broken voice when they were in.

Stacia stroked the plum coloured leather seat. Only for Julia we wouldn't have this, she thought. She would have loved it.

They still had the car in much the same mint condition ten years later when Henry took them to Grafton show. They normally went to the Lismore show but had never before undertaken the long drive south.

Stacia and Monnie loved shows. There were awkward moments.

"How's Julia?" asked schoolfriends when they bumped into them at Lismore show, many with babies, some on home visits from teaching or nursing jobs, some trying to settle back into rural life after years abroad, spent on what they called a working holiday, boasting about their menial jobs in hotels and restaurants or picking crops to finance them for another stage of their journey, though scorning such occupations in normal life.

"We should say Julia is saving for a trip like that and that's why she doesn't come home," Stacia said to Monnie, resting under a coral tree and watching a short, dark, cruel man do public tricks with some monkeys.

He shouted orders to one monkey, but needed to wrench it by a rope attached to its neck to have it obey. It scrambled up a ladder and stared down at the people with dull sad eyes, its head jerked again as a reminder to leap to a board swung between two poles, where aided by another jerk of the rope it was set swinging. Straddling the board, the monkey continued to stare at the people, adding boredom to the dullness and sadness.

"Poor Julia," Monnie murmured and the two of them got up to go to the farm machinery pavilion where they were to meet Henry and Mildred.

Often they passed little knots of Aborigines, who most of the time looked at the ground, rubbing fists against their mouths or stroking their arms. When they'd lift their heads to look through the crowds, they appeared miraculously to see no one. It was the children on parents' hips and shoulders whose bold, calculating eyes met those of the white people. It was as if the children were charged with the responsibility of challenging the whites to insult or belittle them, secure in their belief in equality: children being beautiful and engaging no matter what colour they came in.

A good thing about the Grafton show, thought Stacia and Monnie, was that there were fewer blacks there. A restricted rodeo programme acted as a deterrent, and fewer parties undertook the long trip from towns on the Queensland border, which was more liberally sprinkled with reserves and hamlets and deserted mill towns turned into shanty towns predominantly occupied by blacks.

Stacia and Monnie averted their eyes when passing the groups. They overlooked the obvious: if Julia was among them she would stand out with her white skin and could scarcely be missed. Like Mildred they had a vision of her black too.

"What would you do if you saw her?" Monnie asked once of Stacia. "Would you say something?"

"No," Stacia said. "It wouldn't be what Pa would want."

It was Henry who saw Julia. His exhibit of tropical fruits won him first prize and he decided he would take home a bottle of rum and have a little nip at bedtime to celebrate. On the way out of Grafton he left the women in the car and went into the Clarence Hotel.

From the steps you could see over an iron fence into a little park that ran down to the river. Quite a few people were there, some of them guests at the hotel for the show, seeking relief after tramping the showground, soothed by the sparkling water and the soft accommodating grass, kind to feet pinched by unfamiliar footwear.

Henry saw the comely young woman on a seat, an arm along the back, no so much to rest it as to protect the young child beside her, a girl in a sedate style of dress, a pleated skirt rather long, and a blouse with a sailor collar. She was a terribly fair child, he could not mistake that, her hair was a whitish gold tumbling to the middle of her back.

There was no chance of the woman turning her head to see him. She had eyes only for the child of nine or ten. The little girl had paper wrappings from sweets which she smoothed out on her raised knee, the woman watching the little game with what appeared to be loving indulgence, judging by the curve of her neck.

One of the papers suddenly flew off in a little wind and the child gave chase, the woman rising and bending forward as if she might follow, but sitting when the child caught the paper before it reached the water, and came running back in triumph. Sturdy as she was, she flung herself on the woman, who hugged her hard as if she had been rescued from drowning.

The embrace unsettled their hats and the woman straightened hers, the child taking hers off and dropping it on her head, again drawing Henry's attention to her abundant fair hair.

It was not Julia then, and the child could not be Julia's. She was too light skinned by half. This was bound to happen to him. He had developed this terrible habit of looking into every young woman's face and following every young woman's figure that might be Julia's age. His imagination was getting out of control. He must stop it.

He was nearly back to the car when he remembered the rum. He would not go back for it. There was the risk of looking too long and too hard at the woman and child, who might be leaving the park by now and come face to face with him.

He would tell Mildred the hotel did not have the brand of rum he wanted.

Little Lost Flanagans

The sea lay out in front of the house and the mountains reared up behind. The sea was always changing and the mountains could look different every day for a month, but the house did not change except to grow shabbier. The gate was dragged back one day to let someone through, then rain fell for a week, and the gate lodged in the mud. When it was fine again the grass grew and knotted itself in the wire. In spite of the efforts to drag it closed, the frame resisted, rusting in defiance. It did not seem worth the effort after a while, so the people living in the house, all of them skinny fortunately, squeezed through. Some cows got in and ate everything except a rose bush, which was thick-stemmed and wild and thorny, not having been pruned for a dozen years. The unanimous decision was then to abandon any idea of keeping the front neat. The two older girls and the boy Shannon, aged twelve, dragged the gate open several more inches to give the cattle a more comfortable passage through. This kept the grass down but added to the wilderness with the liberal addition of manure which turned to pads, neat on the ground like round baked mud pies.

The children would sit on the front steps and con-
template them.

"That one's a real pretty green," said Bernadette, the
eldest at fifteen, her eyes fixed dreamily on a fresh pad,
part of it on the path.

"It's like a hat," said her sister Colleen. She looked up
at Bernadette, whose crinkly red hair fell halfway down
her back. "It'd look good on you."

"A cowshit hat," said Shannon. His voice was part
dreamy like Bernadette's. Their father spoke the same
way. He was Irish, but the mother's grandparents had
migrated from Scotland. Their separate origins caused
bitter fighting between them. There were three younger
children named Donald, Jean and Heather. The people
in the little town took an enormous interest in the
Flanagans but had as little to do with them as possible.

The sight of the half opened gate saddened the
children on the steps. It reminded them that it was like
that to let cattle in, not visitors. Mrs Flanagan came out
with a hairbrush to do Bernadette's hair. Bernadette
screwed up her face and winced in advance. "Down on
the other step," said Mrs Flanagan, whose sentences
were short like her temper. It was time for Colleen to
look grateful. She had short, straight, whitish hair that
never tangled and could go for days looking respectable,
hardly needing a comb or brush.

"See the cowshit hat," Shannon said. "You could wear
it to mass." Between strokes hard enough to thud
against Bernadette's scalp, Mrs Flanagan reached out
and struck Shannon a blow on the face. "Wow!" he
cried and felt for blood.

"Wow!" cried Bernadette, for the brush hit her head
as hard as it had hit Shannon.

"I forgot. I thought I was still wackin 'im," Mrs
Flanagan said. "Serves you right anyhow for inheritin'

his hair." Colleen's relief was renewed and prompted her to go for a comb. She returned to her place on the steps and put her head to one side and combed her hair, which swung out like a piece of light coloured towelling.

"After this git down to the beach and see them others are alright. Could be washed to New Zealand for all anyone knows, or cares." Bernadette panicked trying to be still. She pictured the little white face of Heather the baby greenish through a wave, her red hair turned greenish brown like seaweed streaming away. Hurry, hurry. Hail Mary full of grace. She dared not allow her lips to move. Please hurry.

When Bernie and Jean Flanagan married it was because Bernadette was on the way. The Campbells had the general store in Oakwood and though Scottish they were as fiery as the Irish Flanagans. But it was a kind of inward fire, and when all of Oakwood knew what was going on, little fair Jean, only sixteen, wearing her brother's blue drill overalls to try and disguise her thickening figure, the Campbells carried on the same as before, smilingly grateful for custom (which increased in many cases out of curiosity). Mrs Campbell took the horse and sulky to the outlying farms for the weekly grocery order, and Mr Campbell delivered it in the old Ford.

The Flanagans looked after the wedding arrangements, since Bernie and Jean were married in the Catholic church. Mrs Campbell smiled on while she made up the order for Mrs Flanagan of cordial essence, cream biscuits, cracker biscuits, fish paste, aware that it was for the breakfast to follow the service in St Columban's.

"One tin of sardines enough?" asked Mrs Campbell, waving it above the goods piled up on a big spread of brown paper. Living in the town, the Flanagans did not have their order delivered.

"Most adequate," said Mrs Flanagan, deciding a haughty tone fitted the occasion, and this set up titters and giggles from several young Flanagans on either side of her, varying in height from halfway up the counter to a head above it.

Mrs Campbell made her mouth prim and lowered her eyes. She decided to be haughty too. "I hope the weather remains fine," she said. What she means, thought Mrs Flanagan, is that since we'll be eating on the veranda it'll need to.

"We know the right saint to pray to for fair weather, don't we children," she said to the astonished little Flanagans, who were not consistent prayers and had no idea of the saint she was referring to. They were acutely embarrassed too for Mrs Campbell, since they had always believed that only Catholics knew about prayer and God.

Everyone was curious about the Campbells' reaction to the wedding. There was more than the usual run of customers that morning. Although there was a note up: "closed for family reasons".

Jean expressed her gratitude in part to the Flanagans for taking her in by giving the first three children Irish names. Then Bernie was able to buy their own place with a deposit of forty pounds left to him by old grandfather Flanagan and they moved there. Jean felt she was no longer obliged to her parents-in-law. Bernie went away stripping wattle bark for six weeks and in his absence Jean took the children from the convent school and sent them to the public one. The next child, born soon afterwards, was a boy whom she named Donald.

"That'll fix 'em," she said, trying to remember where she had heard the words before.

You might have thought (the townspeople did) that Jean and Bernie would be happier, more amiable towards each other in a place of their own. Not a bit of it. Mrs Flanagan senior had done all the cooking and a lot of the washing for Bernie's children, mending their clothes with a sort of affectionate grumbling. Jean grumbled now without the affection. The extra children and the light bill made them poorer. There was no money to spare to improve the house and Jean resented and resisted the responsibilities she had craved under the senior Flanagans' roof.

Bernie often came home after weeks away, working at whatever he could get like road building, bark stripping, fencing and clearing, and straight away set the two big tubs on the kitchen table, one to bathe the young ones and the other to soak their dirty clothes. Jean would ask for money to pay the bills run up at the stores. (They did not deal at Campbells' but the other general store, fortunately opened the same year as the wedding.)

She nearly always came home with a carton of cigarettes and a haircut. Bernie tried not to mind the cigarettes, but made a big thing of the haircut. "Mum looks good, doesn't she young uns?" he would say to the children, glad for the sound of the cupboard door slammed on the cigarette carton, worried at their disappointment that it wasn't something they could eat like cream biscuits or bananas.

Bernie was away now. He was stripping wattle bark again for a property owner at the foot of a range thirty miles south towards the Victorian border. Bernie was only employed by the man with the contract. The bark was stripped, dried and bundled, and the profits on the sale divided among the gang. He would be home long before his share arrived.

"If he gits a penny farthin' out of it, which I very much doubt," Jean said, a hand under a fall of Bernadette's hair that turned the colour of dark blood. The hair pulled from the scalp brought tears to Bernadette's eyes. Her head was tipped back, her white neck strained, her swallow difficult. If she said a Hail Mary it might have the effect of stopping her mother. But she doubted she could manage it through to the end without moving her lips, and she could hardly expect a prayer to be answered unless it was finished. The eyes of the other children turned in the direction Bernie would come when he returned.

The road seemed terribly empty. It was only visible to them for one hundred yards or so coming up over a rise, ragged at the sides like a long tattered towel laid between two grassy banks. So blank it looked. It seemed no one would ever use it again, least of all their father. And then someone did appear, the young Motby boy, wheeling his bicycle to the top of the rise with lowered head, then mounting the frame, spinning the pedal right way round with the scuffed toe of his shoe, steadying the wobble, opening his mouth, rounding his eyes, pushing his jaw sideways, poking his head forward and tearing down the hill. Whoosh! and he was across the culvert, his backside raised again and his knees coming up hard to take the next rise.

"Bloody show off!" yelled Shannon. Mrs Flanagan brushed a last stroke and laid the hand with the brush between her knees.

"You should have a bike!" It was known she was addressing Shannon.

"I don't want a bike!"

"You should have a bike!" she cried, and reached out and cracked him with the brush. He moved down a few floorboards. Bernadette stood and looked up, eyes crinkled, like her crinkly hair, towards the sea.

"No one's gone to look for them others," Mrs Flanagan said, and gave her knee a few knocks with the brush.

Bernadette sat again and Colleen squeezed close to her. They looked at the sea then down to their laps.

"No one budging?" said Mrs Flanagan.

"Shannon?" said Bernadette, looking at the leafy dead buds from a daisy bush between his big and second toe. He turned his face to the rise in the road where it disappeared.

"No good lookin' that way for 'elp," said Mrs Flanagan. She shifted her feet, and Bernadette used her body to push Colleen further along in case Mrs Flanagan was about to go down the steps. "I don't keep dogs as bad meself," said Mrs Flanagan.

Shannon got up and leapt over the daisy bush and was still looking at the sea. "Shannon's going," Colleen said and put her arms tight around her raised knees.

"Hours too late!" said Mrs Flanagan.

"Donnie and Jeanie and Heather," murmured Bernadette, and she dropped her face on her knees.

Colleen jumped up and stood by Shannon. When agitated, Colleen shook. She had to clamp her jaws together to stop them rattling.

"Stop that silly shivering," Mrs Flanagan called. "What news to give 'im when he gets 'ome," she moaned. "Not that he'll ever care."

The other children turned left to the rise, which was emptier than ever. Shannon sauntered forward, head down, until he reached the gate. He kicked it, then he put a hand on the top and vaulted over.

"There he goes," Colleen said, and came back to the step.

"To pull the little bodies from the sea!" Mrs Flanagan cried.

"You said they were washed to New Zealand!" Colleen burst out crying.

Mrs Flanagan cracked the hairbrush on her shoulder. "Stop your cheek!" Bernadette dropped her face on her knees again and said a Hail Mary, her lips working against her skin, tickling it. "I know what you're gabblin'!" Mrs Flanagan cried, the brush thudding on Bernadette's scalp.

In a minute, the two girls got up and went down to hold the gate.

"If only dad would come," moaned Colleen.

"With cigarettes."

"And money for a haircut!"

A Tale of Good Taste

Ernie Potter worked in the post office. He was short and nearly bald, with a round rubbery face the colour of rhubarb. He had no wife or family and he rented a room with breakfast at Mrs Cossington's, two blocks from the main street where the post office was. It cost him nothing to get to and from work as he could walk. He had never owned a car anyway. Every day for his midday meal he went to the same cafe, one that served old fashioned dishes like roast beef and baked vegetables, curry and rice, lamb stew and bread and butter pudding. It was the kind of food his mother had given him when he was sixteen and started in the post office (not this one). He still missed her, although he was fifty-five now and if she were alive she would be ninety. Every morning of her life she had walked with him to the gate when he was setting out for work. This was when he missed her most.

After his mother died, Ernie moved from her two bedroom flat to Mrs Cossington's. The block was dark red, square, and ugly, with no garden, only a lawn to the edge of the path. The six tenants shared the cost of paying a man who came every second Friday in summer and every fourth Friday in winter to do the mowing. Ernie's mother had given him all the path to walk on in the shoes she kept beautifully shined. Whenever he looked at the edge of Mrs Cossington's brick path with the violets and candytuft and cockscomb spilling over, he got a picture of his mother's thin mauvish mottled ankles balanced on the edge, trying to avoid crushing the flowers but not encroaching on the path, taking care she did not hamper his progress, keeping clear of his briefcase which she shined the same as his shoes.

This morning, Potter became confused thinking of her while he looked at the agapanthus near the gate bunched like giant green ribbons. He imagined her face screwed up with concern at seeing the plants wet with rain and threaded under the gate, wincing at the spotting his trousers might receive.

He got through the gate and started down the wrong way, and the three Perry children on their way to school opened their mouths and turned and looked back in the direction he was taking to see what was attracting him that way. He walked on and saw his mistake and turned to find the Perrys lined up at the side of the footpath, giggling and holding their schoolcases up to hide behind them. Ernie made his back straight and hurried past, scurrying like a stubby cockroach, ruddier than normal. I can't think what . . . I don't know why . . . I can't imagine whatever made . . . And he sweated on until he reached the back door of the post office where Miss Paula Cappell slid the bolt along with a loud rattle and let him in.

All the staff were standing around eating little brown squares of cake, the spicy smell rising above the usual post office smells of glue and ink and rubber and new paper and floor wax, for the floor on the public side of the counter had been done at six o'clock that morning by the cleaner. Potter had never seen her but imagined her looking like his mother, especially when he saw the high shine on the brass handle of the double doors that let the public in and out of the office. The underneath was as shiny as the part that showed. His mother had put two of his old socks on her right hand to grasp and rub the handle of the glass-fronted bookcase in the hall, to get to every part and have it sparkling like one of those crackers the Perry children held when they raced past the house on the Queen's birthday holiday.

The bookcase had been sold with all their things from the flat. Mrs Cossington had his room already furnished. He couldn't ask her to move the stuff out. He had never lived anywhere but with his mother; he could not even remember having to set a bed up or move a chest of drawers. The day he left, his room in the Mosman place was the same as he had remembered it before starting school. He had never known his father, who had died on a ship torpedoed in the Pacific when he was an able seaman in the Merchant Navy.

The people at the post office, curious about the changes in Potter's lifestyle (of necessity) after his mother's death, asked about his personal effects when he was moving from the flat. He shifted on an ordinary work day, taking with him only one suitcase for his clothes. It was a shabby one he was ashamed of as he carried it on the bus and then into the lunch room for everyone to stare at.

"What about the photographs of your father and your mother, perhaps?" asked Miss Cappell, laying a square of cake daintily in the saucer of her teacup, then licking her finger daintily too and lowering her eyes as a mark of respect to his newly bereaved state.

Potter shook his head, licking a corner of his mouth to retrieve a crumb, or perhaps a tear. He had let his father's photograph go with everything else to the auction rooms, and his mother had never had her picture taken. There was one of him aged four, on a rocking horse, which was wooden, as was his expression. His mother had curled his hair in rags the night before it was taken. The curls looked like clothes pegs hanging on his over-fat cheeks. He had watched the man unhook the picture from the wall and fling it on his mattress, dump a pillow on the glass, then fold the mattress end to end. Potter had turned away from the last sight of a corner of frame peeping from the striped ticking.

That day, to mark his move from Mosman to this suburb, Miss Cappell had brought her brown cake for afternoon tea. Now, twenty years on, here she was with her cake again, offering it around before they started work. Miss Cappell had taken it to her writers' meeting the evening before but barely half had been eaten. "One guest writer was a diabetic, unfortunately," said Miss Cappell, laying her slice on a sheet of paper which described in detail the newest issue of stamps for philately. The fat senior assistant snapped his teeth on his slice, grateful for the writer's illness. Miss Cappell dragged a sigh from her bosom, lower and heavier with her advancing years. Her face was darker and riper than her scalp, and the centre parting of her hair whiter, but this was only because her once-brown hair, now dyed black, made it show up. Her figure was thicker, and in a cream coloured tight fitting skirt and jacket she looked like a fat garden grub. The sigh was for her unpublished state, compared to that of the visiting writer who had addressed the group and read from his latest work. Like the others she had tried to look intelligent and knowing, although she had no idea what had gone before or was to come after the chapter he read. "Fresh and exciting," she said, folding the grease-marked stamp brochure into four and dropping it into a wastepaper basket. "I can't wait to get my copy."

Potter ate his cake in some discomfort. His mother had been strict about sweet things. On Saturdays she baked a plain butter cake which lasted for the week. He had a slice every night at bedtime with his hot cocoa. When he was a schoolboy he had cake only with milk after school. (She gave him an apple every schoolday for recess and an orange with his lunch.) He could not remember ever in his life eating cake in the morning. As soon as he decently could he would go to the washroom and rinse his mouth with two glasses of water.

He returned as Miss Cappell was unbolting the door top and bottom to let the little bunch of people in. This was when she would put on her disdainful expression, avoiding looking at anyone's face. She did not hurry to take her place behind the counter, or to push forward the little stand reading *Miss P. Cappell*. She pulled open a drawer for no reason, looked at what it held, then slammed it shut. "Yes please," she said to the first chest pressed to the counter, keeping her eyelids down to hide what her eyes were saying: "But for you lot I wouldn't be here. God I wish I was at home writing."

For relief she transferred her thoughts to Matthew Beck, last night's writer. He was sandy and lanky and shabby as you would expect a writer to be. She had bent down to pick up a dropped coin (being the group's treasurer) and had seen his shoes with a little trim of whitish mud filling the crack between the soles and uppers. They had not been polished in a long time; the punching on the toe caps melted into the soles. But worst of all was the way he had fastened the strap, not putting the end in the buckle but leaving it to cock in the air after he had pushed the prong through the leather.

Remembering, Miss Cappell looked at Potter's shoes,

for he was serving someone with a postal order. They were like two dark brown shining beetles, the polish carried right to the sole and the heels, winking with the shine on them. She looked up his well-pressed trouser leg to his drooping ruddy cheek with the urge to compliment him on his footwear, and on his neatness generally. Perhaps it was quite fitting for a writer to look the way Matthew Beck did, thought Miss Cappell, giving someone a sheet of stamps and scattering the money into the different wooden cups in the drawer, rather as if she was throwing grain to fowls. Perhaps he did a lot of walking, stewing over plots and things. Maybe she would do better if she did the same. She sighed under her woolly suit and looked down and patted her tan silk blouse and fingered her pearl brooch, wondering if she should have worn the ruby, then thinking it would not have gone with the tan of her blouse. Again her eyes fell on Potter's shoes, twinkling behind a wastepaper basket as he rose neatly on his toes to show brown unwrinkled socks, for he was serving someone with private mail from a box high up. I do like a neat tidy man, Miss Cappell thought.

Potter held the taste of Miss Cappell's cake in his mouth all day, even after his tea. Mrs Cossington allowed her boarders space in her pantry and refrigerator for the meals they needed to prepare themselves. He was terribly bewildered by this at first and continually left the milk in the pantry and the bread in the refrigerator. Mrs Cossington got the idea of marking the food with p's and r's and after a time he got it right. It was a few years now since he had had to cut *r* in the side of a tomato and circle the *p* on his jar of pickles. Today he carried a bread roll home in a paper bag and had cheese and pickle on one half and tomato on the other and a glass of milk (he was still nervous about making tea). After sitting on the front veranda with the evening paper for half an hour, he was still running his tongue around the inside of his mouth chasing the cake taste. "Blow it," he said to himself, and took his paper and folded it as if it hadn't been read and put it in Mrs Cossington's magazine holder for the other boarders. He would take a walk. It was an advantage living close to the sea, not that Potter looked that often at the water or sky, noting the changing moods, nor did he admire the beds of cannas and hydrangeas the council tended. He would not even take advantage of the seats facing the best views, for he felt foolish sitting next to strangers. He wouldn't sit in an empty seat and draw attention to his solitary state. If anyone should join him he would want to move away immediately, terribly worried they would take it as an insult but believing himself incapable of starting up a conversation or responding to one the other started.

He was also fearful of meeting other staff from the post office who lived locally. If he was in different clothes from those worn for work he was greatly embarrassed. On the other hand, it didn't appear to trouble some. Probably it was the persistent taste of Miss Cappell's cake that caused him to recall meeting her one Saturday morning while wearing an open necked checked shirt he had bought for weekends. She was in slacks, which the postmaster did not allow on women in the office, and a blouse down around her hips, worn with a wide red belt very shiny like her lipstick. She seemed to be pleased to have him see her like that, but he was terribly self-conscious about his shirt and his little flat paper bags of cold meat and cheese. He feared the carton of potato salad he had fancied at the delicatessen might split suddenly and plop the contents on Miss Cappell's open-toed sandals that had a distinct holiday look about them. But today he remained in his work clothes so if he met Miss Cappell by accident he would not have any worry about his appearance, and he actually had nothing to buy. It was foolish of him to think of Miss Cappell anyway, but it was that cake taste still hanging in there. He would take in big gulps of sea air and that would fix it.

But the cake taste came on strongly when he passed a shop with warm vanilla and coconut and jam smells pouring through the open door. And no wonder. For there was Miss Cappell, studying the window display with a quite pensive expression, her gaze on a squarish, flattish brown cake similar to her own, iced but with a scattering of cinnamon — or was it cocoa — on top. Miss Cappell was thinking about treating hers similarly next time she made it and was trying to decide between the cinnamon and the cocoa when she raised her eyes on Mr Potter trying to get past without being seen. "Oh, you," she cried, emphasising the "you" and causing Potter to blush a deeper rhubarb. Foolishly he looked behind him, but no, she was addressing him. And she had only exchanged her cream wool suit jacket for a loose hip length coat left unbuttoned and with the belt dangling. She wore it sometimes to the office and he rather liked it now he came to think of it. It made him recall with pleasure his grey zipped-up waterproof jacket with the wool collar and cuffs which he would be soon taking out of its clear plastic wrapping from the end of the wardrobe where he stored his off-season clothes.

"Weather's turning cool," he said, closer to her coat than he had ever been and seeing its pattern, large checks in pale greys and creams running together so quietly the pattern was hardly obvious. It was the sort of coat he would recommend if he were shopping with a woman. Goodness me, he thought, wondering what on earth his face looked like since it felt like boiling beetroot. He had only been selecting his own clothes for a few years, as he'd worn those his mother bought him until they wore out, years and years after she died. The boiled beetroot feeling ran right down to his shoes at the idea of buying clothes with someone who wasn't his mother. He couldn't escape redness it seemed, for he looked away from Miss Cappell to the fruit market on the opposite side of the shopping plaza, which was brightly lit and made brighter with the piled fruit, particularly the great pyramid of apples so red and shiny, like baubles beside a pyramid of green ones, shiny too, making Potter think of Christmas although it was more than six months off.

"I need to buy some apples," he said, putting a foot their way.

"Oh, do you?" cried Miss Cappell, delighted. "I said to myself when I saw them (although she had her back to them) 'I'll take Mother some apples.' "

Of course, thought Potter. Miss Cappell lived with her aged widowed mother. "Between Mother and my writing . . . !" Miss Cappell said frequently when asked about her activities away from the office.

Potter bought four apples although two would have been enough, and Miss Cappell said, "Four for me too," causing the girl in the stained green uniform with the cap bearing a red apple applique on the peaked front to wonder briefly about their relationship. She had thought they were a married couple. She served Miss Cappell first although Potter was in the lead. Dear me, I should have ducked behind her, he thought, but giving the girl a deep nod saying it was quite right that the lady go first.

At home he took out his grey jacket, ripped the plastic film off quite recklessly, stuffing it in his waste paper basket, not saving it as he usually did. He raised a leg cheekily and rubbed his apples one after the other on one rump and dropped them in the glass dish Mrs Cossington left in the room for boarders' fruit. Then he went to bed and ran his tongue around the inside of his mouth into the spaces between his teeth trying to track down the taste of Miss Cappell's cake. But it was gone, completely gone. "Well blow it," he said, terribly disappointed.

The Split

Old Mrs Pittman visited her son, Dan, and Dan's little
boy, Gerald, every weekend when Dan had access. Mrs
Pittman hated the word along with a lot of others the
younger generations used freely. She loved Gerald
though, and suffered great misery over a long period
while Dan and Gerald's mother, Roseanne, separated.
That was another word Mrs Pittman avoided. Her
misery increased when anyone within her hearing used it
or the other word, split. Since the split, before the split,
how did he take the split. Mrs Pittman got out of any
discussions starting off like that, and made excuses to
bustle away on some errand, leaving other family
members or neighbours to talk it out among themselves.

She would ask, "More tea, Mrs Hannigan?" quite
sharply, rising sharply too, and when she went away for
more hot water the others murmured that she wasn't
alone with her problem, just about everyone had a son
or daughter — well, split — and it was better to talk
openly about these things. "Indeed, easier to bear when
it is shared," said Mrs Jackman, who had a son of thirty
about to leave his wife, but since there were no children
and he was too far away to visit the units, there was no

cause to mention it. Her daughter coming regularly with her husband and two children kept flying the family flag of respectability.

Mrs Pittman got away as early as was decent on the Saturday mornings. Gerald stayed for the two days with Dan. The split — Mrs Pittman would find another word if it was the last thing she did — caused great disruption to Dan's life. He did not renew the lease on the little restaurant he had on the beachfront, but took a job as a chef for someone else five days a week so that he could be free for Gerald when his turn came to have him, on weekends. Mrs Pittman wanted Dan to give up the funny little terrace house he and Roseanne had bought together that looked like a slice of cake with the roof like icing stopping just short of falling down the side. He could take the spare bedroom in her unit.

Dan's father was retired now, and spent his time at lawn bowls and making his home-brewed beer. He was not too concerned about the plight of Dan and Gerald. Whatever old Mrs Pittman was concerned about almost always failed to concern old Mr Pittman. They had few shared interests when they were young and none at all now they were old.

The day Roseanne left Dan, taking Gerald with her, old Mr Pittman went shopping for clothes. He picked the distraught Mrs Pittman up on her way home from Dan's. She never forgot looking down and seeing his new shoes, a reddish purplish colour on his feet. She couldn't bear to look at them afterwards, and flung them out of sight whenever he left them on the bedroom carpet.

Dan said he would rather stay on in his house and "manage". Mrs Pittman suspected this meant being available if Roseanne tired of her lifestyle with her new lover on a partially settled island a few miles farther north. Roseanne rowed Gerald to the mainland to go to school, and there was a ferry crossing in the afternoon to bring him home. The living conditions were near to primitive. There was only tank water, and only one telephone at the shop on the wharf which was also the post office. Islanders with cars had to leave them parked on the mainland. Roseanne and her lover, Gareth, who was a potter, did not have a car. Gareth had two children by his first marriage that had ended in divorce, and these children spent the weekends with him.

Dan went to pick up Gerald every Saturday morning. He sat in the car watching for the rowboat to grow from a speck to a cork, causing him to pretend calmness until he was able to pick out the small dot that was Gerald, then he'd break out in a light sweat until the moment Gerald climbed in the front seat beside him. "You all right?" he used to ask, until he noticed Gerald's hungry look at Gareth's two children, a boy and a girl, picking their way down the bank to the boat. He gave a strange wan little smile when they sat down sharply, half losing their balance and sending the boat slapping against another. Dan heard Gerald's breath leave his chest, relief, he thought, that the two in the boat were safe. Perhaps he worried getting in and out of the damned boat, Dan thought. Perhaps he wanted to be left with Roseanne to play with Gareth's children. Perhaps he was bored coming to him for the two days. He began to think of the time as terribly boring for Gerald, remembering him at the movies, his expression the same going in as coming out. He tended to shiver violently coming out of the water after swimming, roll himself in his towel with his chin wobbling about over a fold of it, and his frown so heavy Dan didn't know if he was concentrating on other swimmers still in the water or expressing his hatred for it all. He never objected to any of

Dan's plans, like watching the football, or going ten pin bowling, although Dan thought his lightness and thinness was emphasised when he bowled the great ball down the alley, his little body threatening to fly down with it.

When Dan brought him to the house, he had a habit of sitting on a kitchen chair with his canvas bag of clothes on his knees and running his gaze right around the room, making Dan nervous and guilty if he had made any sort of minor change. Since Dan did not take sugar and Roseanne had, he removed the sugar jar from beside the tea caddy and put his biscuits in its place. Gerald stared at the arrangement for a long time, then went to his room, and Dan found him there kicking at the bed leg, which he left off doing when Dan appeared, and began to unpack his pyjamas, swim shorts and spare jumper, then put them back in his bag again, took out the pyjamas and put them on his pillow.

For a few Saturdays old Mrs Pittman went to Dan's place early enough to go with him to collect Gerald. Then Gerald sat in the middle of the back seat for the ride home, and Dan pictured him still sitting in the boat with himself as Gareth rowing it. He kept his eyes on the rear vision mirror for some change in Gerald's expression but there was none. In the end, he suggested old Mrs Pittman just wait at his house and have breakfast ready for them and Gerald could ride in the front seat. She was upset, but it couldn't be helped.

Now she woke early as always, and geared her body for the visit, but had to lie stiffly beside old Mr Pittman. She lifted the little clock from time to time from the bedside table and saw with great disappointment only two or three minutes had gone by.

She gave Mr Pittman his breakfast, setting one end of the dining room table, but she only drank a cup of tea by the sink filled with water, ready to wash up after him. He read the paper, feeling behind it for his toast and cup and pushing his plate just outside the edge when he had finished. I wish it was strychnine, said old Mrs Pittman to herself, taking up the plate.

It was different getting breakfast for Dan and Gerald. She took some parsley from the pot on the laundry window sill and laid a sprig on the tomato she fried with their bacon. She ate only toast and drank more tea watching them eat, wondering about Gerald's breakfast through the week and worrying about Dan's, but reminding herself that little would have changed since the three were together. Dan had always got his own breakfast, for Roseanne was a terrible cook, and Gerald had got his own cereal and she suspected he still did. Poor darling little mite, she thought, watching him lift the parsley between two fingers and lay it on the side of his plate, his brown eyes asking that she not be offended.

"It's just there to make your breakfast look pretty," Mrs Pittman said, apologising too.

"What have we planned?" said old Mrs Pittman, making her voice bright. Gerald looked at his father since he was the planner. Old Mrs Pittman saw Gerald's expression turn sulky, although he fingered the label on the marmalade jar to try and cover his mood. Those times he looks like his father, thought old Mrs Pittman, getting up with her cup and plate and deciding on keeping her back to them while she put water in the sink. Perhaps when she saw them again they would look better. But the little noise of Gerald tucking his chair under the table made her turn. He does everything so carefully, thought old Mrs Pittman. He's so bloody slow, Dan thought, getting up and jerking his chair into place as if saying, show some energy for God's sake.

Gerald looked first through the kitchen door to the back, then the other way towards the stairs.

"Well?" said Dan, his fingers in a rapid dance on the back of his chair. Gerald looked frightened. Then he decided on the stairs and ran for them, his body well forward as if his legs were nervous. Dan pulled his chair out then flung it under the table again, disturbing the cloth and causing old Mrs Pittman to rush and gather up the trembling china.

"He could go and see the kids next door!" Dan shouted. "There should be more for them to talk about, now he's at a different school!" He looked with his ugly mouth as much as his ugly eyes on old Mrs Pittman, who held the sugar bowl hard enough to crush it. "Well, aren't I right?" He gave the chair another shake and then went to the window and sent the curtain flying along the rod with a rattling and squeaking of the rings.

Roseanne had made the curtains, those and the ones in the other rooms. Old Mrs Pittman had shopped with her for some of the materials. Mrs Pittman particularly remembered the ones in the front room, the design of big silver circles on a pale green background. "What do you think?" Roseanne had asked, and old Mrs Pittman thought her face against the green and silver the loveliest and happiest she had ever seen.

For some unaccountable reason she thought of old Mr Pittman's reddish, purply shoes. As unaccountably, she thought of getting home and picking them up from the floor where they were sure to be upside down or on their sides, and giving them a rub with the polishing cloth before putting them away, neatly side by side. Although I mightn't, thought old Mrs Pittman.

The Old Pair

Most people in the village spoke and thought about Jock and Jess Taylor as the old pair. "See the old pair today?" husbands would ask of wives. "Haven't seen the old pair about lately," wives would say to husbands, "have you?" Mothers said to their young ones, "Watch out for the old pair on your way past there." "Both?" asks a petulant child with no interest in the Taylors. "One will do," soothes the mother. If one of the old pair was alright then the other must be.

That theory was established as firmly as their title of the old pair. They had been married a long time. On the sixth of July 1980 when they had been married for fifty years they got a card, the front covered with a painting of wattle in bloom and the word 'congratulations' inside in gold, overprinted on more wattle. Their daughter-in-law Maisie, whom they disliked, had sent it. She was the wife of their son, Bob, and the reason for the couple's living in New Zealand, thus depriving the old pair in their small inland town in the north of New South Wales of regularly seeing their grandchildren, who had been given the outlandish names of Remy and Carlos.

"What's that in aid of?" Jock asked after he had

inspected the card, let the envelope fall to the floor and spun the card by its corner to hit the wall above the fireplace and fall behind the tea caddy. "On the spot" he said, pleased with his good aim.

Jess would have liked it to fall in the firebox. "Damn wattle," she said, stuffing the stove with enough wood to burn their flimsy little place down. "Bring it into the place and you bring bad luck too."

She filled a kettle so full it flooded the top of the stove, and there followed a great angry hissing and steaming so that every crack in the stove was turned into a scarlet stripe. "That's me eyes causin' that! See you bastards, see!" She sent the blind at the window over the sink flying high but it made little difference, for a crepe myrtle had been planted too close to the house and rain had plastered blackened leaves against the glass. Cobwebs billowed and blew like sheets on a clothesline, pinned as they were to each corner.

"Your eyes crook again?" Jock asked, turning his rocking chair to avoid the full force of the stove heat.

"Still. What's wrong with you?"

Jock put an arm over a shoulder to pluck at a shoulder blade. His features ran into each other with his grimace so that they looked like a drinking mug shaped like a face. "The old back." He brought his arm back to run the hand down his thigh and circle his knee. "The old knee." He stood and make a circling motion with a hand on his stomach. "The old gut. Churnin' away there." He opened his mouth and worked his jaws about. "The same rotten taste in me mouth."

Jess dragged a chair to the other side of the stove, and bent her lean old body forward and jerked it, then realised she was on a kitchen chair. "There. Me mind's goin'. I thought it was me on the rocker."

Jock steadied his rocking and held the sides as if preparing to rise. "You want the rocker?"

Jess turned her skirt back to warm her knees.

"If I wanted the rocker, I'd be in the rocker," she said.

"You would too."

Jock rocked and Jess swayed sideways in time and watched the heat bring a shine to her kneecaps and mottle the skin of her thighs. She had worn stockings the same way for fifty years, stopping short of her knees. She pulled them full length first, stretched the top, and rolled the surplus into a knot which she tucked inside the top. When her skirt rode high, the two little knots neatly showed below her knees. The stockings were lisle and the colour of strong tea. Jess's sister sent her three pairs for Christmas every year from Brisbane.

The only children to visit the house, daughters of Jock's niece, were mystified at the way the stockings stayed up. Being girls of ten and eight they tried treating their socks the same way, playing at a game of being the old pair.

"Let's be the old pair!" the younger cried and the older rushed in with, "I'll be old Jess!" and the younger said, "No, me. I'm the youngest and the wife is always the youngest."

The fact was, Jess was the elder. By nearly ten years. She didn't belong to Badgery as Jock did so the locals never knew her right age. She had come to teach school there in 1930, when she was nearly thirty. She did not look more than twenty-five, especially alongside Badgery women with tribes of small children and out-of-work husbands. Her jaw was well defined and her forehead high under a cloud of wild red hair. Old Mrs Taylor, Jock's mother, said once that red-haired people carry their age better, and seeing the question in Jock's eyes said no more. Her boy at twenty was taken with the city girl, who was different from those in the Badgery post office, general store, bakery and hotel.

On Saturdays Jess walked up or down the creek for miles and Jock came upon her one day gathering different coloured leaves from the bank of poplars his father had planted as a wind break. She apologised for trespassing, which amused him, for no one ever asked permission of an owner to take a short cut through a property. Even the Robinsons' children walked through the Hardys' place, though the two families were the bitterest enemies in all the district, since a Hardy was suspected of murdering a Robinson. The Robinson had disappeared during a wild storm preceding a flood. The Hardy man, who was in love with the Robinson's wife, had volunteered to look for the missing man. It was universally believed he had found him and thrown him into the flooded Badgery Creek. The body washed to sea and was never recovered.

The day Jock met Jess under the poplars was the day he first glimpsed her rolled-up stockings. They sat together on a log and a yellow poplar leaf floated down and stayed in her hair and she didn't notice. He liked it there, looking beautiful against the deeper red, and kept pretending to look up to see more leaves falling, envying the leaf snugly settled in Jess's hair. It looked a trifle smug as well, he thought, seeing the wind blowing some strands of hair about making it more secure.

He plucked it off when he was behind her going down the bank to the creek bed. He didn't think she felt it but she did, and was startled and slithered on some damp moss, then leapt even before the slither had stopped across a running stream, bubbling away there clear as glass on the stones, reddy brown and yellow, the colour of the leaves. And her hair. The leap showed the stocking tops, the little rolled bun and some white thigh.

When he was home — and he got there surprisingly fast — he passed the clothes line where the bloomers of his mother and sisters were blowing dry. They were filled with air, striding out as far as the pegs would allow. He stood and watched. His mother came to the back veranda. "I came across the teacher by the poplars," he said. She started to reply, "You should have brought the cows back with you." Instead she said, "It would've been manners to ask her back for afternoon tea."

But the two of them, young Mrs Taylor and old Mrs Taylor, did not get on. The place was big enough for them all, but Jess was restless there. She did not like housework and, worse, did not like old Mrs Taylor organising her. "She's been handin' out the orders for so long she's forgot how to take any," said old Mrs Taylor of the daughter-in-law she had looked forward to with great eagerness. Alma and Annie, the Taylor daughters, felt kinder towards Jess then, although they had made up their minds to leave the farm and seek work together in Brisbane now that Jess was there as company for their mother. They went, but so did Jess and Jock — to a house in the village they rented for a few years then bought. They never moved house again. The change did bring on Jess's pregnancy, old Dr Barton having told her that she would have a better chance free of the dominance of a mother-in-law, the doctor having courted old Mrs Taylor himself for a brief period when he was home on holidays from medical studies. Then, she was Pearl Brown, the storekeeper's daughter, and a better horsewoman than all the other girls born and bred with the smell of horses' sweat in their nostrils (but too bossy by half).

Jess worried terribly about her age when the baby was coming. All the women she knew had half a dozen children or more by the time they were thirty-five. "Thank goodness she's not around me now," Jess said to herself, letting the little house turn into a mess of unmade bed, wood flung untidily on the hearths, and a tin dish filled nearly all the time with dirty crockery. As well as neglecting the housework she could put aside the knowledge of her true age. "I was getting that way I was thinking there was only ten years between us every time I looked at him," Jess thought, deciding she liked the lighter strip of sandy hair above her right temple now that she wasn't constantly trying to disguise it. The old priest who married them was nearly blind and didn't see her age on her birth certificate and she didn't let Jock see it. "How old are you really, Mrs Taylor?" the midwife shouted to her above Jess's screams and the rattling of the iron bedhead in Jess's tormented hands. Jess laid an arm briefly across her eyes. "Thirty-five," she whispered, and thought, it makes no difference, I'm dying anyway, and that'll look better on the coffin.

It was odd that she was remembering this when the back door rattled. "Who's that?" Jock asked, putting his head up fox-like and looking back to the door that opened from the outside onto a cluttered room intended as a veranda but closed in now for a dining room. Since Jess and Jock couldn't be bothered with formal eating it had the dog's dish on the floor, two or three pumpkins, a scarred enamel dish of beans too old and tough for use, and a broken chair where Jock threw his macintosh when he wasn't wearing it. The door took the full force of bad weather and it seemed the wind and rain had teeth that chewed gaps in the wood at the bottom, but there was the advantage of callers being identified by their feet without opening the door.

This looked like Harry Gillespie's old elastic sided farm boots, although he was living in the town now and had given up his place to his son, unlike Jock who couldn't interest Bob in the family farm and sold up. Bob (influenced by his wife) had taken his share of the money to New Zealand where he put it into a fleet of tourist buses and lived with Maisie and the children close to Maisie's family. "Anyway I'm glad they're not around with us growing old," Jess said to herself.

Harry Gillespie was there to tell the old pair that Tom Collins had died the night before in his sleep.

"Old Tom Collins eh?" said Jock in a voice that made the news sound as if Tom Collins had won a large sum of money or a marathon sporting event.

"You taught him school," Harry Gillespie said. His eyes on Jess reminded her of the bits of broken blue china she had spread on a stump as a child playing at housekeeping. The stump had been bleached a whitish grey too, like Harry's skin.

Jock got up from the rocker when Harry had gone and slapped a hand on either side of his chest. "We might go to that funeral."

Jess took a handful of potatoes from the bucket and threw them on the kitchen table. She would scrub them and bake them in the oven and not waste all that good heat. "But what about all those things wrong with you?" she asked, hunting for a knife to cut out the potatoes' eyes.

"What about you? Them eyes? You'll need them. To read the name on the coffin. And other stuff."

"They'll see all I want them to see," Jess said.

Inseparable

Pauline and Alison Downs were inseparable. Pauline was the mother, Alison the daughter. The child didn't know her father but this was not a great handicap, for it was estimated at least half the children in her class at school belonged to a single parent family or had a stepfather or stepmother.

"Ugh!" Alison said of stepfathers, giving her red hair a vigorous shake, showing the underneath part coloured like the sap from the pale trunk of a giant gum tree.

"I'd hate one!"

"Of course you would, my darling!" Pauline said, very happy to hear it. Pauline's work and Alison's schooling were all that kept them apart. Alison was born when Pauline was seventeen, so Pauline had no formal training for a career. She had been working in a variety of jobs since Alison turned five, choosing those with hours that allowed for generous time with Alison.

She had managed on a government pension for single mothers until Alison went to school. This was augmented with money she did not have to declare from doing ironing and cleaning at very cheap rates. All this will change when she's old enough for school, Pauline had said to herself, stacking fresh linen in old Mrs Harley-Green's hall cupboard with ears strained towards the back of the house where the baby Alison was asleep in her folding pram. Old Mrs Harley-Green, who walked about the big house all day with the help of a stick, did not like Pauline bringing her baby with her to work.

One day Pauline, hearing the tap of the stick cease, had gone to look and Mrs Harley-Green was using the point to pull the blanket from Alison's face and look at her. The cold wood touched Alison's cheek and she woke, and Pauline cried, "Don't!" and rushed for her bag and wheeled the baby out of the back gate and to the tram stop, the whipping winter wind drying the tears on both their cheeks. I'll never go back there, never, never, she cried to herself, only partly comforted by the kindness of the bus driver, who held her elbow to sit her down after he folded the pram up and put it by him in his fenced-in driving cabin. But old Mrs Harley-Green sent her car and driver/gardener next day to bring Pauline back, and said she would allow the baby's pram inside until the weather got warmer. I'll stay then until she's crawling, Pauline said to herself. And did.

When Alison was five, Pauline moved back to the district, which she called Harley-Greenville, although they saw nothing of old Mrs Harley-Green. She had always liked the look of the groups of children going to school there. Back in her rundown suburb, where she had rented a bedsitting room with shared bathroom and laundry, her street backed onto a railway line. The rush of the trains made the old wooden house shudder, and Pauline shuddered with it.

"I want us to hear the sea in bed of a night," she said to the four-year-old Alison, who lifted her face to take this in. That forehead, Pauline said to herself, admiring its width and whiteness, made whiter by the crown of red curls. You can see it thinking.

As well as wanting to hear the sea at night and walk by it in the daytime, Pauline wanted a better environment for Alison. If she did not move away, Alison would go to school with the children who hung about the paling gate, sores on their knees, their dresses too long or too short, shirts without buttons, too big or too skimpy, in the hot weather their things too heavy and in the cold never warm enough. No, no, she said to herself, avoiding the plea in Alison's eyes to join them and, clasping her closer, telling her they would go down to the back fence and see the trains go by and wave to the people inside. Those people were going away from this place to somewhere better, she kept on saying to herself. Where we'll be going. The best she could do, though, was two rooms and bath at the rear of a house at a minimal rent, with the proviso that she go through the owner's place daily, washing the breakfast things, dusting, making their bed and tidying up generally.

The couple were in the fashion business and went abroad two or three times a year. It only took Pauline an hour most days to "run through" the Redmans' house. There were no children and if there was any undue untidiness it was from swatches of material or new clothes waiting to go back to the factory and flung about on settees and chairs. "Oh you gorgeous smelling things!" Pauline would say, laying a cheek on the silk or wool, sometimes a fur trimming while folding them and laying them beautifully on the spare room bed.

Mrs Redman was small with a lot of black curly hair and dressed as you would expect in extreme fashions. Mr Redman was small too, with hair the opposite from his wife's, cropped so close it was hard to decide what colour it really was.

"What colour is Mr Redman's hair would you say?" Pauline asked Alison whilst doing hers, and thinking there was no other hair in the world as beautiful. "Fawn?" said Alison. "A sort of greyish fawn. Like a cat's fur." And she giggled, then turned the giggle to a "Wow!" since Pauline had tugged a little hard, pulling the comb through the red mane from the crown to the end tips, reaching Alison's sharp little shoulder blade. She was ten now and they had been in Harley-Greenville for five years.

"We will never call it anything else but Harley-Greenville, will we?" Alison asked Pauline in their bed where they did most of their talking. "Do you think Mr Redman is a full man?" she continued without waiting for an answer to the previous question.

"What do you mean a full man?" Pauline replied, although she had a fair idea of what Alison meant. She delighted in hearing Alison out, discovering the direction of her thoughts. "Oh you *know*!" Alison said, and turned over to bite Pauline's shoulder, which was naked, for she wore a summer weight nightdress with thin shoulder straps though it was now late May.

"You should have a warm nightie," Alison admonished in an adult tone.

"I could leave my gown on if I liked."

"Get a new gown too."

"Next winter."

"Oh you've been saying that since I was a child."

She took a little bite and giggled. "But Mr Redman," she said, swishing her hair around like a bright curtain at a breezy window as she raised her head and caused Pauline to clutch the blanket to her neck.

"Remember my near nakedness!" Pauline cried.

"Imagine a naked Mr Redman!" said Alison. "What a horrifying sight!"

Pauline had a vision of him, of his shoulders quite wide in spite of his small frame, his chest harp-like with the ribs rippling under the skin, the track of hair stopping at his waist, starting again below his navel, thighs slim but not puny, a strange mixture of strength and weakness. "An odd bod," she said half to herself.

"He'll never be a father, I reckon," Alison said. "He hasn't got the look of a father."

Pauline had another vision. A boy of eighteen, his profile cut out of the darkness above her, sitting up, giving signals that he wanted to go, his clothes back on, buttoned neatly, fussily, even his shoes laced (so they both matched). He seemed disapproving of her, in no great hurry to put her skirt, blouse and shoes straight. His silence made her feel all the guilt was hers. He stood up to take a comb from his pocket and do his hair, its redness lost to the night. She stood too, and watched his back twitch to get his coat straight. "I'm ready then," she murmured, but felt that he would have gone without her anyway.

Ah! but I have you, she said to herself, turning over to wrap Alison in her arms and Alison, as she usually did, wriggled down into the chair Pauline made of her body and thighs. They were quiet to hear the sea. When it was rough it sounded like furniture being moved, or a house being built. "That's a big piece of timber dropped," Alison would say when a wave crashed. "Or the woman was sick of the wardrobe against that wall," Pauline would answer. There were times when it swirled like water in a dish. "There's pebbles at the bottom of the dish and someone is rinsing them out," Alison said.

"The sea's going to sleep tonight," Alison said now.

"It's whispering to itself." They listened to the whisper.

"Something it ate for tea was nice. Hear it smacking its lips?"

"Yes, I hear," Pauline said.

"What do you think Mr Redman would look like in swimming trunks?"

Only occasionally Pauline was late home from work and Alison was there before her. Pauline's latest job was in a sandwich shop in the very small industrial part of Harley-Greenville. The shop opened at ten a.m. and closed at three-thirty, serving food to factory workers between those hours. As you would expect of Harley-Greenville the industry was of a refined nature, a milliner's, laboratories making health pills and skin lotions, and a leather factory. Pauline liked the smell of herbs and honey and lemon from the laboratories and the wet bush smell from the leather place. What great good luck I got this job, Pauline said to herself, quite often hurrying down the side to let herself in and begin buttering bread from the loaves delivered. The ovens were turned on to heat the pies and pasties, and the till was opened, ready for Mrs Baxter, who owned the shop, to tip in her calico bag of change. Pauline's other job was to bring in the flat box of cakes that came with the bread and set them out in the showcase for customers to jab the glass with their fingertips pointing out those of their choice. The flurry of sandwich making started as soon as Mrs Baxter opened the door.

"Cheese and tomato on brown!"

"Tasty cheese or the other?"

"Tasty!"

"Roll or sliced bread?"

"Ham on brown roll!"

"Pickle or mustard?"

"A small flavoured milk and a packet of cigarettes."

"What flavour? What kind of smokes?"

Pauline liked the rush but not Mrs Baxter, who was overweight and dyed her hair to the colour of a bright gold chocolate wrapping. She had no children and Pauline was sure she was jealous of Alison.

Mrs Baxter paid Pauline "from the till"; it was far less than Pauline had a right to, but since Pauline did not have to declare it on her claim for a single mother's pension, she felt she was better off this way. She was nervous most afternoons in case Mrs Baxter found a job for her, like unpacking goods or cleaning out the refrigerators, or polishing the glass of the showcase which was often smeared with marks from the overalls of the boys, whose clothes were soaked from lifting and splashing great cans of lotions in the laboratories.

Mrs Baxter found a job for her today. The cigarette man was late, and Mrs Baxter had lost several sales with people asking for cigarettes first, then when she didn't have their brand going off in a great rush to the shopping centre in the main street where they also bought their sandwiches. Mrs Baxter abused the man roundly when he arrived almost on closing time. Pauline, anticipating Mrs Baxter's request, was wiping off the showcase. Now her overall was off, revealing her red dress with the tartan vest, a style Mrs Baxter couldn't wear but wished she could; it was clearly admired by the cigarette man, who gave only half an ear to her tirade. When he revved up his truck and took off as cheerful as he was when he was on time, Mrs Baxter told Pauline she had better get back into her overall and give the benches a good scrub down while Mrs Baxter made out cheques to meet the bills. There was still a week to go before payment was due but it gave Mrs Baxter an opportunity to complain at the low profit of late and to express doubts that she could carry on "the way we are" for too much longer.

Pauline ran home worrying more than usual that Alison might be there before her, because it was sports afternoon at her school and sometimes the class was dismissed half an hour ahead of the normal time. She saw her waiting outside the locked house, a man in a car slowing down, getting out and scooping her up, a hand over her mouth, the car speeding away. No, No! No, No! And she rushed, pressing into the knot of people at the street intersection, earning curious looks, especially from schoolchildren, who wondered at the odd behaviour of adults running without a schoolbell commanding them. Pauline saw the children too. They are alive and safe. Is she? Is she?

She was. She was on the little balcony above the garage, the terrace as they called it. No railing, for there were no Redman children to keep from tumbling to the pavement. Alison was in a reclining chair and Mr Redman was in a straight backed one, with his legs across the table, a small round one with wide apart slats like his chair. He usually sat in the reclining chair. Pauline knew how Alison had always admired it, and, though she had never said so, wanted to sit in it. Alison had her elbows out, each on a blue and white striped cushion and her red hair spread on another and her young legs stretched out reaching only halfway to the end. Pauline was angry. Jealous and angry. She stopped herself in time from calling out sharply that she was home, and though she walked normally down the side path to let herself in neither Alison nor Mr Redman appeared to hear.

I have told her, I have told her a thousand times if I have told her once, we don't have anything to do with the Redmans apart from what I do in the house. I don't have time to sit down, much less sit on their chairs. I have time for nothing but work.

Unpacking the half loaf of bread and slices of ham from her basket, she saw her hands, red from scrubbing the benches. She wanted to cry at her nails. They appeared swollen, like ugly fish scales.

She hadn't put rubber gloves on for the scrubbing because she didn't want to waste even a few seconds getting away. She hooked her string bag on its nail by the window and flung that open. Alison and Mr Redman saw and heard, and Pauline heard the skittering of chair legs as they got up and came to the edge of the terrace to look down on her. "Mum!" Alison cried. "Mr Redman likes the sounds the sea makes too!"

"When you come, bring the covers from those cushions for me to wash," Pauline said, lowering the window, which was foolish, since she had just opened it for some air. She managed to keep even the smallest tremble of anger out of her voice though.

A Lovely Day

The day was like a newly bathed baby. You would almost expect to hear it chuckle as a baby does when tickled with the towel. It had the fresh smell that soap has and a sprinkle of powder scented with lavender. A steel grey cloud had opened a slit of an eye and beamed some orange light on the houses packed together on the eastern hill. The gardens looked fresh from a bath too, which was not all that surprising because there had been a heavy dew. The tops of the shrubs were smeared with a fine netting, as if someone had dipped a brush in a bucket of cobwebs and painted over them.

Very few people were about so early, but those that were sparkled too. The milk truck had finished its run and the clang of empty bottles had a merry ring. That's it, that's it, they seemed to be saying, and the boy who helped on the run before school swung his legs over the back, his head poked out from under the half raised shutter. He looked eager to get home to breakfast and just as eager to get into his school clothes and dash away with the cut lunch his mother made him. There was a young woman on her way to catch an early train in a long red skirt with bold grey checks, red stockings and

red shoes that went slip, slip, slip on the pavement. She
had a big black shiny leather bag swinging from her
shoulder, which she held in place against her body with
a white hand and fingernails painted a bright red.

Watching from her front porch little Mrs Kerry
Carew, who was only twenty herself, thought the girl
might have bought the skirt, shoes and bag the day
before, which was Thursday. When Mrs Carew had
gone to work Thursday was payday, and the day the
girls bought new things or got them from lay-by, and
Friday was the day everyone looked a little smarter than
earlier in the week, perhaps to celebrate the start of the
weekend or in some cases to start it with an evening out.

It was silly the way we all tried to outdo each other,
thought Mrs Carew, watching the red girl disappear into
the busy part of the street, taking a little of the day's
brightness with her.

She was on extended leave from her office, compas-
sionate leave, said the report Mr Unwin wrote for head
office. How wonderful to have the leave without the
compassion, thought Mrs Carew, shaking her dark head
with the four red curlers in the front part to make it fluff
up nicely when she dressed to go to the hospital. Her
thoughts ran on as they frequently did imagining Colin
fit and well, going to his job as an insurance clerk, and
her with all those wonderful hours free to be a
housewife. She wouldn't be bored, dear me no. Instead
of kissing him goodbye while he was eating his toast and
reading the paper, for he went to work later than her
and in a different direction, she would be on the other
side of the table eating a proper breakfast, not needing
to dash to the bedroom and make the bed with her cup
of coffee and toast on a paper napkin on the bedside
table.

She would never be one of those wives who complain-

ed about husbands reading the paper at mealtime. Her
Colin earned any small luxury he could get, having a second job at a restaurant waiting on tables, then working
in the kitchen when the last customer left. He wasn't
usually home before three o'clock in the morning, but it
made no difference at weekends, he was up well before
seven to get on with the brick paving at the back, filling
in the L-shape between the kitchen and laundry doors
where they planned to have mandarin and cumquat trees
in white tubs.

In fact she liked looking at the bit of his head that
showed above the paper, his forehead wrinkled right up
to where it went under his hair, and the way his hand
went up to sweep the hair down in the curve he liked.

But of course now. . .

His hair now. . .

Little Mrs Carew needed to shake this vision off and
take on another Colin working with the bricks. Now
that's better. Pushing a brick down into the soil as far as
it would go, grunting and hitching up his old shorts.

"Stop for a cool drink, darling," she would say.
"You'll wear yourself out."

"Just let me finish the row."

His hands now were light as a moth's touch at her
wrists while she held the glass for him to drink. Then
back on the sheet, his eyes turned from them, ashamed
at their uselessness.

Little Mrs Carew was thinking she really should go inside and start dressing when Mrs Beck from next door
came out in her red dressing gown to collect her rolled
up paper from the lawn. Mrs Beck was old, nearly
seventy, and so was her husband. This was the first
home of their own, as they had lived all their lives in
bank houses in western parts of the state. Whichever of
the Becks went for the paper unrolled it, and not yet

having put their glasses on, turned to catch the strongest light holding the page at arm's length. They read the death columns first which used to amuse the young Carews.

"Good heavens above," Colin once said, burying that page of his paper behind the sports part. "They're looking for who's got there before them, poor old things." Then he went straight on in a scandalised voice reading about a player in the football team he followed being unfit for the next game. Little Mrs Carew failed to see the importance of it but assumed a sympathetic expression as she pushed his lunchtime sandwiches into a plastic bag.

Mrs Beck caught sight of Mrs Carew and crushed the paper in a guilty way under her arm. "How is he?" she called.

"The same I guess as last night," Mrs Carew said, putting an arm up, for the sun was suddenly quite dazzling. "Isn't the day lovely?"

"Yes, indeed," Mrs Beck said, giving it a slightly disapproving look.

The telephone rang from inside the Carew's house. Mrs Beck mutely pointed the paper at the side window, indicating the telephone's temporary place on the end of the dining room sideboard. The Carews had planned to get a little table for it with a drawer for the directory and space for one of the potted plants that Mrs Carew had a talent for raising.

Mrs Carew could see Mrs Beck didn't want to go inside without finding out about the call.

"That'll be Mother," she said, rushing away. She held the phone to her ear for two seconds without speaking. Then she said: "Hullo, Mother!" There were two more seconds of astonished silence.

"You knew!"

Mrs Carew felt as if she had been dry and burning hot, then a wonderful cool wave rushed right over her. "I was just sure it was you." Mrs Cresswell didn't ask how, or mention Colin. She said she was going to Manning's big linen sale and suggested Mrs Carew meet her in the foyer of the shop and they could have a bit of lunch in the cafeteria and see if there were any good reductions in curtain materials.

"They might have just what you want for your front room," Mrs Cresswell said.

"You mean our living room," said Mrs Carew, as she usually did to try and bring Mrs Cresswell into the present. Mrs Cresswell used the language of her own newly wed days, and it was quite absurd, for the Carews' front room was the bedroom and had curtains of soft rose to match the rose and beige down-filled quilt the Carews had snuggled joyously under before. . .Well, not for some weeks now.

Then Mrs Cresswell said: "You can go from there to the hospital, and if you like I'll go with you. Or if you'd rather . . ."

"I'll see how he feels this morning, and I'll let you know when I see you at Manning's." Little Mrs Carew had nearly begun to cry. She was like that lately. When people asked about Colin she wanted to shout angrily at them how could he be any better than the last time they asked, which was most likely as recent as the day before. Then when they didn't ask she couldn't concentrate on what they were saying waiting for them to, and hating them for their callousness. Mrs Cresswell obviously had him on her mind. Mrs Carew's heart, so full of love for Colin, spilled some towards her mother. I mustn't be sharp with her when she comes out with that old fashioned stuff, she decided, pulling the pins from her hair on the way to put on the apricot wool suit she had worn on her honeymoon.

When she closed the front door behind her she saw Mrs Beck by the dividing fence with three new roses in one hand and a sheet of tissue paper in the other. "Take him these," she said, and as little Mrs Carew put out her hand for the roses her phone rang again. Oh dear, said the stricken face of Mrs Beck, what is this one about?

"It's Mother again," Mrs Carew said, laying the roses on top of Colin's clean pyjamas in her raffia basket. "She forgets something while we're talking and calls right back after she hangs up. She never fails."

"I could hold your things if you want to run back," said Mrs Beck, her creased face on the window as if she thought the phone might oblige them by leaping out.

But Mrs Carew shook her fluffed-up fringe and said whatever Mother had to say could wait until she met her at lunch time.

And she hurried through the gate and out into the lovely day.

At the Curnows

Everyone visiting the Curnow family knew that sooner or later the little Curnow girl would come into the living room and climb onto the bottom tier of the blackwood table in the corner by the piano. When she began crawling at the age of seven months, she swept away the fat family Bible that had been there for dozens of years and climbed up (although it was a tiny climb since the tier was only a few inches from the floor). Her mother, Grace, found her rocking her little body back and forth and called everyone to come and look. There was quite a crowd in the end — the baby's father, her grandmother, two uncles and an aunt, plus the aunt's best friend spending the Saturday afternoon there. There was also the young brother of the friend and it was on him the little Curnow girl focused her attention.

He fell on his knees by her and put a hand on the little pink foot with its row of tightly packed toes resting on the carpet. "Oh look, how sweet!" cried Nancy, who was the aunt and felt she had been partly responsible for the charming little tableau. The little Curnow girl, whose name was Julie Rose, looked everyone over with an expression that plainly said she had no use for their adoration if that's what it was. She had a particular scorn for the grandmother, who took her glasses off and blew on them and rubbed them with a corner of her grey silk jacket, frowning not at the task, but at the sight of the Bible, upended and looking like a tent blown over in a gale. The best friend picked it up and laid it on the chiffonier, keeping her eyes on Julie Rose. "Oh, she looks like a Dresden china ornament there." She clasped her hands together and then wrung them. "That's what you should have there."

"A Dresden shepherdess figurine would go the same way as the Bible," said the grandmother.

Grace scooped the child up and held her tightly, swinging her about to emphasise the grip on her. Her eyes, china blue like the child's, took everyone in except the grandmother. Bob, the child's father, sat down on the chaise longue to put on his cricket socks which he had in his hand when his wife called. Grace sat with the child on the big hooked rug (made by the grandmother) in the middle of the room and with great tenderness put the little girl on the pattern of climbing roses on a brick wall. Little Julie Rose turned at once and crawled to the table and hoisted herself onto the shelf and beamed around at them all. "She's made a place for herself there alright," Bob said, turning down his sock top.

She had too. The Bible never went back there, Julie Rose grew taller but there remained enough head room and even leg room when she bunched her body up under her chin. Her feet then curled over the edge and her grandmother, now more or less spending all her waking hours in her big chair, rapped the arm with her stick. Since she did this whenever she wanted attention, it did not bother Julie Rose, who just watched the door for someone to come and slipped her feet onto the floor when they did. Everyone took the part of Julie Rose, so old

Mrs Curnow would have to ask if the mail had come or what that burning smell was or who had been on the telephone when it last rang — particularly if it was Grace who came, with her "Yes mother" and her eyebrows climbing up under her hair and her hands being wiped almost frantically on a kitchen towel. Grace's mouth was mostly part open, showing her teeth longish like the palings of a picket fence. She concentrated on the wiping, waiting for Mrs Curnow to say what she wanted. Often Mrs Curnow didn't. For Grace would begin to show her teeth more catching sight of Julie Rose, with face raised angelically towards her and toes turned inwards on the carpet. "Oh look at the sweet rose. A jewel of a rose that's what it is! Yes, a precious jewel!" And she swooped upon her. Julie Rose put her face playfully away, pressing it through one of the little openings like glassless wooden window frames joining the top tier of the table with the bottom.

Once when Julie Rose was out with her mother, old Mrs Curnow, alone in the living room with Bob (her son), pointed her stick at the little table. "See how worn the bottom part is and the edge scratched where she puts her feet? She's getting too big to play there."

"A few bumps will make the thing more valuable!" Bob said. "The place's full of old junk. Good to see some of it getting some use, now don't you agree with that?" And he stretched out on the chaise longue and caught up a cushion between his two feet, tossed it to his hands and stuffed it beneath his head. "This thing doesn't get any softer."

"For all its use," thought old Mrs Curnow.

Bob opened one eye on her. "They bred 'em so tough in the old days they made their furniture to match!"

They knew what work was too, said old Mrs Curnow to herself.

Grace came in with Julie Rose. They had let themselves in by the back door so that Grace could leave her
basket on the kitchen table. "No one has washed up the
lunch things," she complained. Bob swept his feet to the
high back of the chaise to make room for her to sit. Julie
Rose trotted to sit her little rump on the table tier. She
spread out her legs in their white socks and new red
shoes. "Look Papa," Grace said, and Bob lifted himself
to turn and look. "New shoes!" he cried, and lowered
himself again. He turned his face so that he could keep
the shoes in his line of vision without sacrificing his
comfort. He took Grace's hand and plaited his fingers in
hers. "Oh beautiful wife!" he said, kissing her fingers
and some of his own.

Old Mrs Curnow closed her eyes so that she wouldn't
see. When she opened them the little red shoes were
balanced on the edge of the table tier and the little gold
coloured face of Julie Rose was squashed between her
gold coloured knees.

"I was just saying to Mother all this old junk should
go," said Bob, shutting his eyes. "Don't you agree,
beautiful one?"

"Wall units are all the go," said Grace, her eyes on the
wall above the blackwood table, causing Julie Rose to
crane her neck in that direction, allowing her feet to fall
to the floor with a klunk.

Like red shoes, I suppose, said old Mrs Curnow to
herself.

"Where is everyone?" asked Bob, pulling Grace down
to lie partly beside him, partly on top of him. Old Mrs
Curnow turned her face away. He is not asking me
anyway, she said to herself.

"Where are we? That's more to the point," said Grace,
using her picket teeth to bite his shoulder.

I don't want you here, don't think I do, said old Mrs

Curnow, her eyes edging towards the picture of her late husband, Robert. She heard the little table creak with Julie Rose rocking it.

Bob swung to a half-sitting position, pulling Grace up and leaning against her. She leaned towards him as if they needed the support of each other.

They look like two fence posts tumbled together and that's all that's stopping them falling over, thought old Mrs Curnow. The rest of the fence is gone.

"We could do one of two things, Mother," said Bob holding the hand of Grace very tight.

Could you indeed, thought old Mrs Curnow. As if I wouldn't know what they would be. Julie Rose put her face through one of the little openings.

She hears better that way, thought old Mrs Curnow. But Julie Rose pulled her face out almost at once and leapt to her feet, the little red shoes twinkling on the hooked rug.

"Here comes Aunty Nancy!"

Nancy came with a basket over her arm filled with material the colour of buttercups, light and silky. Nancy's long white hand spread among the folds as if they needed to be held to stop them ballooning away. "Look!" said Julie Rose, pointing to her shoes. Nancy dropped the basket and pulled out the half-made dress, hers to wear as bridesmaid at the best friend's wedding. She held it to her with an arm across her waist. "My shoes!" said Julie Rose stamping one of them.

"My dress!" cried Nancy.

My home, thought old Mrs Curnow.

A Henry Lawson Story

The worst thing you could do for Mrs Lil Warwick was to give her an outing. Mrs Warwick had a lot of children and a husband, Clem, a man who unlike his wife enjoyed outings. He was something of a leader in their little town, although he was the smallest merchant and his house was not in the best position. It had not been painted or repaired in more than twenty years, which was how long the Warwicks had been married.

Clem's father had opened the town's only grain and produce store and Clem worked with him from the time he left school at the age of fourteen. He was lucky. An only son, he was left the business when old Warwick died. Clem did what most young men of the town did between the two world wars, married a local girl, first making sure she really was pregnant.

Lil's obsession with staying at home started then. Her mother insisted on what was called "a proper weddin'". Lil stood and sat through it in her satin dress and tulle veil feeling terribly foolish and ashamed. She faced the day as an accused man would, believing there was life after execution.

After the wedding, Clem and Lil went to the south

coast for three days. Lil sat on the beach in the blue and white check dress her mother had made her, the hem lower in front, ready for her expanded stomach to drag it up level with the back. She watched Clem swim. Isn't it funny, she said to herself when he was ready to go in, standing with his back to her in his bathing suit, that is the most undressed I have ever seen him. She blushed and pulled the lowered hem even lower over her stretched out legs and thought, only tomorrow to go and we will be home.

Clem was glad to get home too. He had started to take an interest in local affairs and had been elected that year to the Agricultural and Horticultural Show Society, and would probably be the treasurer at the annual meeting after the show in March. Lil did not go to the show.

"You're married," said Lil's mother. Lil, blushing at the painful memory and standing back from the kitchen table while washing up because of her belly, was startled to realise she was. She worked all day in the house and yard, got Clem's meals ready on time and sewed four nighties, three matinee jackets, a dress and three petticoats for the baby.

"I can find plenty to do here," she said, and when she came inside after pouring the washing up water around the roots of her young lemon tree, she began taking the crockery from the dresser to wipe the paper lining over and put it back so neat and ordered, with the big plates on the bottom, the saucers on the top and the cups stacked one inside the other, so that they looked like a display in a china shop. "We'll sit on the front veranda in the sun and I'll start working some flower clusters on the jackets," she continued, sitting her work basket on her generous hip.

Out the front, the two Rankin women, Annie, respectably married and expecting, and her sister-in-law

Alma, respectably occupied as a stenographer in the town's one solicitor's office, slowed their steps passing the Warwicks', and Lil stopped hers halfway down the hall. "The back's sunnier," Lil said.

Lil's mother thought Lil would be better with the second child. She imagined her tucking the first, a girl, into the back of the pram and giving the rest of the room to the new baby, stopping to let people admire it, going to the shops on Saturday afternoon or to the tennis like other young matrons of the town. But in her infrequent walks, Lil, though pleased with the boy and dressing him with great pleasure in a crepe de Chine smock with a blue duck embroidered on the left side of the yoke, would turn the pram away from the town and push it along the road into the bush. There was more than a mile of walking with little risk of meeting anyone. There were only three farm gates opening onto the road, the fourth farm at the end belonging to the shire president, Councillor Fisher, and his brothers.

The Fishers had more than one car, late models that went very fast, the driver concentrating on the ruts and bumps. Since the road was not a public one, its cost and maintenance had to be met by the farmers. Councillor Fisher, with his reputation for integrity to uphold, did not dare to err too far on the side of favouritism when the council made its allocation of money for road works.

Lil would push her pram to the extreme edge when there was the noise of a Fisher car, glad it wasn't a Watts or Allan or Perry, who had early models that fumbled their way along the scantly spread bitumen, giving time for an exchange between driver and pedestrian. Lil had to nod to the Watts, Perrys or Allans, for they were customers of Clem's. Little Shirley shrank back into her corner staring with fear into her mother's face. "Gone now," Lil murmured, pushing on. "Gone, all gone." She was soothing herself as much as the child.

Some years later, there were two different children in the pram, both boys — Trevor, aged three, and the baby, Ronald. Trevor loved cars and didn't object to people.

"Ah, see that!" Lil cried when a Fisher car flew past. She turned to watch and smiled her widest smile. Lil had a nice smile. She had a large rather droopy face and cheeks like a pair of soft pillows. The smile split the pillows as if a head had suddenly found their beautiful use.

Councillor Fisher this day caught the smile in his rear vision mirror. "Ah! see that!" he said aloud although he was alone, and reversed the car, a very new Ford, with a violent slither to stop next to Lil. She gripped the pram handle in terror and could not raise her eyes higher than his right shoulder, a nice firm one in tweed.

"A nice day for your walk," said Councillor Fisher lifting his hat. Lil saw a brown wrist, gold cuff links, and a piece of very white sleeve. She put her hip against the foot of the pram, her mouth working. She thought of a water tank, the water below the level of the pipe connecting the tap, the water breathing and sucking, desperate to reach the opening. Councillor Fisher sped away touching his hat again.

Trevor tried to stand up in the pram and make a noise like the car engine. "Zephyr!" cried Lil, having read the lettering on the car's rear. "That's a breeze!" She lifted her face as if there was one blowing towards her, and smiled again in welcome.

Councillor Fisher saw and almost reversed again. "Oh, no I'd better not!" And he drove on. My goodness me, it is a lovely day! he said to himself, racing the car through the shadows thrown by the trees. It hit a rut and bounded on to the gravel filling a gaping crack, a recent so-called repair job by the council's road gang. That wouldn't do, by George it wouldn't do. He had an instant vision of Lil stopping, tipping the pram, putting it across the crack, stepping across, not seeing the trees or the sky or the birds, the wretched road taking all her attention. I'm too humble by half in regard to that piece of road, too humble by half, so I am, he said to himself, the Zephyr moving gingerly along now.

Councillor Fisher frowned down on the patches of crumbling bitumen, even the leaves and twigs from the giant gums. Some of those big trees should be lopped, that lantana cleared; it would spread across the road before long and become a harbour for snakes. He would have a few words to say at the next works meeting about the allocation of money for maintenance of roads like this one. Farmers couldn't be expected to wreck their vehicles and meet the high cost of replacing tyres. People were using the road for walking too, some quite regularly, a very pleasant walk it was too. Not everyone used the park (which was named Fisher Park in honour of Councillor Fisher's efforts over several years to have it built). Some liked solitude. He was rather that way inclined himself.

His thoughts then turned to the Henry Lawson story of "The Drover's Wife" he had read as a schoolboy. His favourite story. That woman, little Mrs Warwick, who never went anywhere with her husband and had most of her shopping done for her by her mother or bought from catalogues (he opposed this practice of not supporting local business but approved in the case of Mrs Warwick, who really was consistent in her desire to be alone) made him think of the drover's wife, whom he would have liked for a mother. He used to see himself killing the snake for her, then flinging himself on her bosom and being nursed and rocked. Councillor Fisher's mother was a different kind of woman. She was a hospital matron who never gave up working and he and his brothers were brought up in the quarters built for staff. Councillor Fisher had always wanted to know if she had loved his father, who was killed in World War I, but he had never asked. Councillor Fisher had no wife himself.

Brown and Green Giraffes

George Carr mourned for a suitable time following the
death of his wife, then began to think a lot about a suc-
cessor. George had only one child, a daughter who was
high up in education, as he expressed it to anyone
asking, who lived in Canada. She was married to a
Canadian, also high up in education, and together they
wrote books on teaching methods. Barbara came home
for her mother's funeral, distressed that she couldn't
stay longer than a week because she was giving a paper
at a conference in Calgary. As it was, she had to change
times with another speaker and would arrive late at the
conference. She had worked right up to the time her
plane left, making neat little asterisks on a pile of pro-
grams ready to go to the delegates, drawing their attention to the change, explaining on the bottom margin the
reason for it.

"I insist," she said. "I feel less as though I'm letting
everyone down."

With George in the living room after the funeral she
offered puzzling compensation for letting him down by
leaving so soon.

"I'll take the fruit girl," she said, sweeping a figurine

from the mantlepiece, a girl with a basket of fruit on her hip. She said she would have it touched up by the experts at home in the more culturally advanced country, and George saw with a deepening depression the shabbiness of the porcelain ornament when moved to a new light. When Barbara then carried it off to pack it among her fashionable clothes he felt he should move the other things on the mantlepiece to close the gap, but didn't think he could manage this and was miserable as he thought of looking at the space for the rest of his life.

But when he came home after taking Barbara to the airport, the space was filled. Mrs Oates from next door had let herself in to leave a macaroni cheese on the kitchen table and pick through the flowers from the funeral. She had made new arrangements of those still fresh, some cream roses among them which she put in a brass jug, and made the mantlepiece look quite different after forty years with the fruit girl there.

George found the macaroni still warm, and although it was only eleven o'clock in the morning, hardly lunch time, he sat with the dish on his knees and ate, staring at the roses.

"A woman's touch," he said aloud. "There's nothing like a woman's touch." He dropped the empty dish in the sink with such a klunk he snatched it up again and ran his hands around it looking for a crack.

In the bedroom he took off his jacket and as had been his habit all his married life flung it on the bed, wondering at the difference there. Usually the quilt was on smooth as a billiard table as Jess made it, then Barbara while she was home.

"Gorblimy," he said and went to look in the second bedroom where Barbara had slept. He pulled the quilt back and saw the pillow naked of its slip, the blankets turned back on the mattress.

George looked stupidly for sheets, and even looked over the bed end at the floor.

He remembered then seeing Barbara early that morning on her way to the laundry with a great bundle of something coloured green (he thought). He went there and looked about him. A big white washing machine, above it a dryer, the door of which he opened, feeling surprise that nothing was inside. Nothing in the washing machine either, he saw when he lifted the lid. He removed the lid of a wicker basket. There were the sheets looking as if a plum pudding was inside them.

"Blimey," he said looking at the neat arrangement of packets and bottles on a shelf and below it a line of books from which hung brooms, mops, dusters, dustpan and brush. He saw there were curtains at the small window with a design of giraffes on them, long-necked brown giraffes, some very silly-looking with half their legs off or a rump missing where the material was cut and hemmed. The curtains were familiar to him although he never went into the laundry. Although he had always thought the giraffes were green. Then he thought, ah, I've got it, and trotted to the kitchen where, yes, similar curtains hung above the sink except that the giraffes were green. There's nothing slow about you George, he told himself, and went to the living room to sit in his chair and stare at the dark grey face of the television and think about the curtains. He imagined Jess shopping for them. She couldn't decide between brown and green, he supposed. He had always thought of her as a silly indecisive woman and here was proof of his intelligent judgment. Then he remembered she was dead and he should be charitable. He decided to think of her as clever, taking a colour for each room when she was unable to choose between them.

She knew how to spend the money, no doubt of that,

George thought, then had to pull himself up again. In guilt and some confusion he switched on the television and stared for a while at a demonstration of raising African violets, then switched off and wandered to the window to look out on Jess's garden.

This had been her main hobby. He would sometimes come from golf or a business luncheon (although retired from the taxi company where he was secretary for thirty years he was still a shareholder) and find her, a stoutish woman in a grey skirt and green jumper, pressed between the shrubs working furiously with a digging fork.

She could sprout something herself, George often thought, mildly irritated that she might have neglected dinner preparations. Of course she hadn't. In the kitchen he would see her little shiny tightly lidded saucepans of vegetables ready on the burners, and since he watched his weight and favoured grills, the steaks would have been thawed on the enamel plate, lapped gently by their own bloodied juice. In a little while she would be in, her gardening gloves gone, a big flowered apron over her jumper and skirt, her large arms shaking their flesh as she lit the gas and turned the saucepan handles inwards as she had done since Barbara was a year old.

He could never understand how she could have everything ready at once, even the baked custard warm the way he liked it. He went to the kitchen now and stared at Mrs Oates's dish with a yellowish crust formed on the inside. He should fill it with water, he supposed. Or wash and dry it and take it to her. She might then ask him to eat dinner there. He stood in the middle of the kitchen with his hands in his pockets. He was incapable he knew of removing them to wash the dish, incapable of drying it. He searched the room for tea towels but could see none, the steel rack above the stove was emp-

ty. They must usually hang there for George had never
seen the bars exposed before. He tugged at the green
giraffes and yes, there they were outside spinning on the
clothesline. He should bring them in he told himself, but
he had never done such a thing in his life. He looked
nervously about him as if there was a danger of his
thoughts being exposed to an onlooker.

He sauntered through the house to the front in time to
see the afternoon paper spin through the air and land on
the stone floor of the porch. He picked it up, shaking it
free of leaves, thinking they were not usually there, and
started to think why they were allowed to be and switched the blame quite quickly from Jess to Barbara.

She had always been a selfish girl, her mother doing
everything for her while she was at school and university, then allowing her to go off overseas when she had
been teaching for only a year, and all that money spent
in bringing her home for her marriage to that fellow Edward who had never heard of the Melbourne Cup. He
didn't come out for the funeral as he should have done,
so that they could have stayed for Barbara to look after
him as it was proper for a daughter to do.

Back inside he looked into the double bedroom which
he had supposed they would occupy, while he would
have the other room. He picked his jacket up and laid it
down again and felt renewed irritation with Barbara,
blaming her for the tangle of blankets and sheets as if
she and Edward had passed the night there and she had
failed in her duty to make the bed. It would not be a
good idea though to have Edward here. He wouldn't fit
in, not liking golf, football and fishing, and never having heard of the Melbourne Cup.

Perhaps Barbara would come back alone. She could
well be deciding that on the plane at this very moment
and would be back before he had dirtied all the crockery

in Jess's cupboards and used all the sheets in Jess's linen press. He made his way to the living room slapping his thigh with the paper.

A few weeks later he was there again in his chair, a board on his knee backing a pale blue sheet of paper he was filling out. He was up to the question How would you describe yourself? Careful/generous. George looked at the vase of dead roses on the mantlepiece in place of the figurine. "Generous!" he said aloud. "Very generous!" But he didn't write it down. George knew women. There would be some who would not stop at brown and green giraffes. Just think of all the other colours giraffes could come in.

Snow White and Rose Red

The two daughters of Mr and Mrs Sam Bacon each had a child, Laura a boy and Beth a girl. Neither daughter was married.

When Laura had Sebastian Mrs Bacon was quite put out, but recovered and carried on like a normal grandmother. The other one won't inflict that on us, Mrs Bacon thought, with a mind picture of Beth's dark sharp face and narrow body. Beth wore very colourful clothes, red stockings with black shoes, or black stockings with bright blue boots and skirts that were bright enough in themselves without the addition of colourful panels which made Mrs Bacon think of a parakeet darting about in the orange tree. Beth was never satisfied with a band in her thick black hair, vividly coloured as you would expect, but also tied a scarf with the tails flying out behind.

Laura was different. Pale and quiet. Snow White and Rose Red they were called as children. It was Sam who thought of that. Sam kept on calling them Snow and Red, which Winnie the mother did not really approve of, but she was happy that Sam was so happy with the girls. He never mentioned a desire for a son and seemed indeed to have no interest in boys and, Winnie suspected, was quite sorry for those who had them.

Then Laura in virginal white, a long linen skirt and a cotton blouse heavily trimmed with lace, beige sandals, and toenails painted a pale pink, said she would be having a baby in the coming September. The first thought that flew into Winnie's head was "Spring! How appropriate!" (She was the kind of woman who liked order and propriety in all things.) Then she had to tell herself how wrong! How terribly wrong! For Laura was without husband. She wasn't even engaged. As far as Sam and Winnie knew she wasn't even walking out with anyone, a term she and Sam used only between themselves.

It was Winnie who burst out crying. Sam felt confusion, thinking it should be Laura crying, since she was the one in trouble. Beth came into the room looking at the faces one after another. This had been arranged, Sam could see. Even Winnie raising soaked eyes knew that it had been organised for Beth to appear directly after the announcement, not during or before it. Winnie's eyes had flown first to Laura's white waist, then went to Beth's. She was in faded blue overalls such as farmhands wear (and belonged with them, Winnie thought) and a great red shirt blousing out under the arms. She looked like a red poppy in full bloom.

Winnie wished she could drop the habit of looking at waists when an impending birth was announced. I'm so old fashioned, she thought. And looked again at Laura's middle because she couldn't help it. And then at Beth's. She won't do that to us, she thought.

But Beth did. Sebastian was not a year old when Beth visited one Saturday and began by saying, "Now, Mother, no hysterics please. We went through all that with Laura." She's a hard, cruel girl, Winnie thought, already with a handkerchief pulled from her jacket pocket. She held it crunched on her knee and raised woeful eyes to Sam. "Tell me it's not true," they said.

Some noises came from the side veranda. Laura was there putting Sebastian into his pram for his afternoon sleep. He gave one of his little shouts, not angry, not playful either. A warning that while they went ahead with their plans he may have some of his own. Beth jerked her body forward stiff on her chair as if she would go to him. Then she settled back and let her face say she knew. His little leg would be thrown outside the covers and his head flung from side to side on the pillow and nearly all of a little rubbery hand in his mouth. His eyes would be flashing about, slate grey eyes, an unusual colour for a little child, beautifully shaped too and with lashes a lovely pale brown, lighter in colour where they curled.

"Who else in the world has eyelashes two different colours?" Laura had cried out when she was nursing him one day a few months before in Sam's big chair, and Beth as it normally happened was visiting too. She had come with her Roger, who was married but separated. Roger was standing by Winnie's chair and Beth was in it. Winnie was wondering if they expected to be asked for dinner and even when she left them and went to the kitchen, opened the door of the freezing cabinet in the refrigerator and stared inside at her bundles of chops and rolled roasts, she held in her mind Beth's face and the way she gripped Roger's thigh and how he looked down and studied the hand. Beth looked everywhere except at Sebastian, but Winnie believed she held him in her head just as she herself was holding Beth in hers.

She had returned to say there were four big steaks. She could halve one with Beth, who talked a lot lately about becoming a vegetarian, and if they didn't mind dinner a little late to allow the meat to defrost a bit, they were welcome to stay.

Only Laura and Sebastian had stayed.

When Beth visited to tell Winnie and Sam she would be having a child in the coming winter (Winnie too distracted this time to associate the event with the season), Roger was not living with her any more. Her beatific expression over her coming child had disturbed him, made him think a lot about his two-year-old, and sent him back to it and its mother.

"It would never have worked," Beth said, flinging a rug she was knitting with sudden energy into a new position on her lap. Winnie felt the gesture also flung Roger from her forever. She started to feel glad about this for she did not like the way his eyes couldn't meet hers for the start of a conversation. They waved away as if someone had flapped a sheet at them. But it meant Beth was alone as Laura had been (and still was). Winnie watched Beth's hands working with the wool, black and dark grey and rust, and thought it was terribly unsuitable for a baby's bed if that was what was intended. She will probably wear it as a skirt until it goes on the bed, Winnie thought, rounding her eyes to keep them dry and noticing as Beth gave it another fling that there was a great bird in the design with spreading feathers sharp as the points of knives. Winnie turned away from it.

The little girl Sarah slept under the blanket in a basket on two chairs in a corner of the gallery where Beth worked. Customers at times thought the rug was part of the art and craft on exhibition and went to spread it out for a better look, startled to find the child there. The rug was beautiful but Sarah was not. She had trouble keeping food in her stomach and stayed lean, but not frail. Winnie thought she would look better if her skin was not as dark, like the colour of light tan boot polish. The darker hair had a wet look, lying in spikes on the baby's forehead. She thought Sarah was the sort of baby Beth would have. "You wouldn't get anything pink and white and cuddly from her," Winnie said to Sam.

Sam did not think Winnie should have that attitude. He was so concerned he put aside his embarrassment at his beloved Snow White and Rose Red with children and no husbands, and the discomfort of explaining them to his golfing friends, to make a fuss of Sarah and atone if he could for Winnie. Now he was walking up and down the living room with the small brown spidery thing trying to wrestle out of his arms. Sam's chin was held back as far as it would go, for he was smoking a cigarette and with no free hand was keeping it in his mouth at an angle where the ash would not fall on the baby. He grasped her feet when she was rubbing one against the other as if she was bent on removing the skin. "Her feet are cold! Feel them, Win." Sam laid his cigarette carefully on the edge of an ashtray to concentrate on wrapping a large hand around Sarah's feet and holding them to his baggy old grey sweater. "Cold feet give babies bellyache! Get me a blanket to wrap her in, Win!"

Win handed a plastic elephant to Sebastian, spinning the wheels on which it sat, and watching his little hand go out as it always did to stop the spin. She looked away from Sebastian on a folded tartan rug (neat and sensible) to Sarah's legs, moving up and down in a bid to wrench the feet free of Sam's grip, and thought of the pink bootees she had knitted for Laura and Beth which she did not dare offer for Sarah.

Beth then returned from a trip to the shops, closed the

front door, and laid a canvas bag of groceries and
vegetables by a chair leg. Her enormous patchwork skirt
reached the top of her boots and she flung away a cloak
that appeared to Winnie to have been made of pieces of
a soldier's greatcoat joined with black darning wool in
blanket stitch. "Has she been the goodest girl in the
whole of the world?" Beth asked, clapping her hands
and opening them to take the child from Sam. She sat
and pulled up the front of her jumper and from its black
folds drew a brown breast, the nipple brown too, quite a
dark brown, and Winnie thought that it at least should
be pink, and watched unhappily as Sebastian got to his
feet and pattered across to stand by Beth's boot and
stare. Beth lifted the baby and turned her to the other
breast so that Sebastian's stare was fixed on the back of
Sarah's head. Laura came from the back of the house,
having filled Winnie's clothes dryer with Sebastian's
things taken from Winnie's washing machine. Beth raised her eyes to Laura. "She's so terribly active for her
age. I'll soon have to feed her completely alone." She
returned Sarah to the other breast and screwed herself
away from Sebastian's gaze.

"Come, my darling," Winnie said, and scooped him
to her and backed to the lounge to sit and encircle him
and the plastic elephant in both her arms.

Laura sat by them and held Sebastian's leg. She gave
it a shake. "Old Placid Pot here could eat anywhere!"

Beth's eyes rested briefly on him. "Yes, I can believe
that," they said. Then with a great sweep of her skirt she
carried Sarah off, and they heard the heel of her boot
close the door of the second bedroom where Winnie
tried to store the bags and bundles they brought when
they visited.

Winnie sighed with the sigh of the bed springs, for she
knew Beth had not removed the things carefully, but

allowed them to slip to the floor, or she was lying with Sarah on top of them. "Give Grandma a great big kiss," she whispered to Sebastian, clamping her chin tightly between his soft shoulder and softer neck. Sebastian kissed her furtively, then slipped from her arms and sat on his rug nursing his elephant. "Oh, such a good, good boy," Winnie said in a moany, singsong voice.

Laura gave her hair a shake and with nearly closed eyes adopted the same part moaning voice, "It would not be possible; it would be humanly impossible to find a better child anywhere." More slow shakes of the head, the voice still moany. "I am so lucky, so terribly lucky!"

Beth's hard boot heels beat the carpet on her way back to them. She had put Sarah into red and black check overalls. She held a handful of the fabric on Sarah's chest to save her face being swallowed. "Go on bootifull," she said waggling her nose on Sarah's. "She's talking. At four months she said 'Mumma' plain as day! 'Mumm-ar', she said. What does everyone think of that?"

"Mumma!" Sebastian called, stretching out a hand with a finger pointing first at Laura then at Beth.

Winnie caught the hand and held it near her face.

"Really we should go," Beth murmured.

"We could share a cab," Laura said.

Sebastian started a leap from Winnie's arm and she gripped him hard. Laura stood up quickly, reached for him, and squeezed and kissed him. He put a foot out towards Winnie for her to tie a trailing lace.

"Car!" he said importantly.

Laura laughed. "We'll walk," Beth said. "She'd rather," very careful not to look at Sebastian. She knew his eyes were on her, asking why she didn't like him.

An Angel's Tome

The plan could only be kept a secret for so long. Jim Angel — what a good name for an author! — gave notice to his employer six weeks before he and his wife Beverley and their two little boys were due to occupy the cottage they were renting for a year in Bobbinook, a village one hundred miles south of Sydney.

"London next!" cried one of their friends, raising a glass of wine at the dinner the Angels gave to announce their departure. They were going in two weeks, their Sydney house was tenanted by a couple of teachers who were pleased to get it, and the Angels had decided to tell everyone at once (everyone being couples from the tennis club and others they met locally, mostly through their mutual dogs and children).

Jim (he thought he would use A.J. on his book) worked for a small publishing firm that put out trade magazines. He had been plotting his book for a year, and had written several early chapters. He had been given a grant of money from an arts board of the Australian Government to finish it. He could not expect the firm that had employed him for ten years (he was only twenty-seven) to hold his job open for him, but he should find a job soon enough when the year was up (a year! it seemed like forever). Andrew Bennett, his boss, had said to call him as soon as he was back in town.

One of the farewell dinner guests raised the subject of life for the Angels after their year in the country. Jim felt terribly sorry for Philip Hill in his dead-end job with the Water Board. Imagine the offers that would follow The Book. There would be a clamour for film rights, a television series, and there were all the contacts he would make with newspapers and journals when he took some short breaks from his main job. He could see his accompanying letter. Dear Sir: As a recipient of a Government grant of money to complete a novel, no cross that out, major novel, no cross that out, major literary work, major literary work, he repeated liking it very much. I am wondering if you would be interested in the enclosed. I stumbled upon it almost by accident and think it is the kind of out-of-the-ordinary, off-beat stuff your journal could present so well. He got those kinds of letters occasionally at work from characters who enclosed pieces Angel found utter rubbish. He never used them or paid for them. Now he would most likely send a few piles off to Bennett.

Dear Andrew: The enclosed is a piece I stumbled across and thought would go quite well (go quite well! It would be the best thing the useless prick had come across since Angel had left him) in the brick journal. Even hardened old me got quite a thrill stumbling on a chimney stack nearly as old as Australia itself. The old guy in the hat down to his shoulders has never had his photo taken before. But read on, the story tells all . . . He could imagine Bennett hurrying to Rosa Pratt in his old chair (the fool to give the job to a woman) and flinging it in the brick tray with one of his spinning gestures, as was his habit when the news was good. Angel would just give old Rosa time to do the layout, send the story with the rest of the rubbish to the printers, and the galley proofs would just be back when he would write to Andrew again. Sorry old chap, but you will have to kill the chimney stack piece. The fellow came banging on my door at two o'clock in the morning. Typical country clot, he didn't wake up to the fact that the media everywhere in Australia would latch onto the story. The chimney is in fact a monument to his Aboriginal ancestors, and is on sacred tribal ground. I want to use it in my book, well camouflaged of course, but that has nothing to do with this request to kill it. He would not hesitate to sue. My shoulders are broad! This should reach you in time for Rosa to pluck something from her file of standby stuff. Standby stuff! What standby would that dopey female have! God, what a laugh.

He was in bed after the dinner party and there were noises of Beverley finishing up in the kitchen. Actually Angel did laugh, taking his pillow from behind his head, shaking it and putting it back, and Beverley came in to see his lips pulled back over his teeth and his grey eyes with a glitter in them under his grey clipped hair and his beard not smooth, bits sticking up. Whatever had made him laugh was not really funny she thought, beginning to worry about how much he drank.

"They were all so grateful that we told them all at once!" Beverley said in front of the mirror brushing her hair, which lay in two deep curves on her cheeks then fell straight down her back from the little clip at the nape of her neck. A good style for the country, with the nearest hairdresser most likely miles away and she never using one anyway. "You know, they felt no one was given preference!" He lay back on the pillow, the glitter gone from his eyes, and a drowsiness there that had little to do with sleep. "I thought it all went off very well." I won't say more, I am getting nervous, she thought, brushing her hair at the back, which was quite stupid since she was about to lie on it. "I liked the way Helen said 'London next!' " She got into bed, "It will be, too." She put out the light by the switch at the back of the bed. Her elbow touched Angel's head only lightly but she nearly said sorry.

"Who is she married to?" he asked. Oh, I am so silly to let it bother me, she told herself with that stupid pain, hardly a pain at all, pinching her breastbone. She cleared her throat to cover a silly little hiccup.

"Sean. You know, he coaches the soccer." Sean was the one who had proposed a toast to Beverley and called her a brave and wonderful lady. She would dispose of Sean (though she wouldn't mind lingering on the tenderness of his mouth, which she had noticed for the first time that evening), and repeat a suggestion of Jenny Rapp's that she should think about taking the floor rugs, her treasured collection of hooked rugs made by her mother and aunts. The country house would probably have only wood floors or cold linoleum. "That sounds a good idea, don't you think?" Beverley said to the centre light near the ceiling, like a blob of blancmange in the near dark.

Angel was awake; he turned his pillow over. "I rather think not," he said.

She waited, and he did too. The silence said, come on you simple-minded nong, let your mind for what it's worth go back a bit.

The quiet went on. There might have been the whistle of a breath.

"You recall the day the agent brought those people. Right?"

"Of course." Voice don't quaver.

"They asked if the floors and window blinds and curtains — stayed. Right?"

"Of course. Right." No quaver at all.

The pillow went over again. Punch. There was enough light from the street lamp for the silvery blob that was Angel's head to rise then fall. Like a wave caught by the moonlight, Beverley thought, feeling a chill as if water had touched her.

She would write to her mother: Dear Mum, Would you do me a very great favour and send (detailed) instructions on how to hook rugs. I will have a lot of time on my hands in Bobbinook and am thinking of making several, particularly in the evenings when Jim is working on his book. I am going to ask my, no our, friends for scraps from their sewing boxes and spare wool, even old good quality clothes I can cut up. So much excitement ahead. If the book does well it could mean Jim writing the next one in London. I can see my lovely rugs brightening up the gloom of a London flat in winter. Then she had the odd, quite ridiculous idea of ending with "your brave and wonderful daughter". How silly that would look. She turned her pillow over for sleep and thought the country would probably be very good for her sanity.

The Rose Fancier

Some said the Parker sisters were in their nineties, but whatever their ages no one was likely to find it out from them. As young girls living in the same house they occupied now, their mother had taught them (along with fine embroidery, water colour painting and how to play the organ) that a lady's age was her own personal and private affair.

Petula and Viola were the sisters. Pet and Vi. As girls Pet was plump and pretty, Vi bony with thin hair and a big chin. At dances, Pet was popular and Vi suffered terribly because the boys didn't rush her and her partners were usually what the girls called, amongst themselves, the leftovers. Even when Vi got one of the sought-after boys she went stiff and danced like a wooden doll, worrying because she couldn't find things to say, worrying because she was sure he only wanted the dance to be over and get on to the next with Pet or one of the lovely Larkin girls. Oh, hooray, hooray, Vi would think, catching up her shawl and bag to take her seat again, wrapping herself in the shawl, feeling as if it were bedclothes and she could go back to sleep now the nightmare was over.

In a little while though, watching the dancing, her misery would return. She thought of the remains of a scarecrow her father finally pulled out and burned, and how pleased she was to see it gone, so she could rest her chin on the windowsill of her bedroom and admire the unblemished sight of his rose garden.

Mr Parker was a rose fancier and had given the whole of the back garden over to a quarter acre of them. He staked some of the new ones, pulling out the stakes as they grew and spread. This pleased Viola too. The men on the dance floor reminded her of the stakes, the girls the roses. Viola at her window liked the way her father tossed the stakes onto the brick path that separated the garden beds. The path went right through to the fowl pens. The wind and the rain made music of the rose garden, and if Viola closed her eyes at the dances she fancied she was carried there, and the notes from the piano and violin on the stage were actually the brushing of rose leaves against each other and the rain tickling the labels Mr Parker tied to the bushes. Viola would cut the labels from an empty kerosene tin and write the name of the rose in her best handwriting with a darning needle from her mother's work basket. Ping, ping said the silvery tin to the rain as it splashed on them, giving the tin a brigher shine and making Viola's fine handwriting show up even clearer. The smell there was sharp and sweet too, more pleasing than the smell of powder and scent on the matrons chaperoning daughters at the dances and the fumes of kerosene from the hanging lamps. Hurry on tomorrow, hurry on, Viola would think.

The garden was a ruin now.

Neighbours complained to a distant cousin of the Parker sisters, who accordingly sent a man to clean it up. His name was Tom Dillon. He didn't know about the bricks. Viola watched while he dug one up and threw it to land near her feet. Viola thought the brick, a lovely dark plum colour, looked as surprised as Dillon, who drove his fork into the earth looking for more. He said there were probably enough bricks there to repair the crumbling front fence and they ought to bring a bulldozer in and tear them up with the old roses, grey and knotted and thick of stem, never having been pruned in seventy years or more.

"What year was them roses planted, do you know?" Tom Dillon asked Viola.

For answer she picked up the brick and hurled it towards Dillon's open mouth.

"Gawd's struth!" he cried and ducked.

"What?" cried Petula opening her bedroom window and putting her round white head out.

"Nothing!" answered Viola, tilting her grey one back and hurrying up the back steps. "See to the stove!"

She always told Petula to see to the stove. Petula never reached it, forgetting when she was half way there what her mission was. She did not leave the window this time, being about to when Dillon began throwing tools into his wheelbarrow quite savagely.

"Hey, you won't be paid!" Petula called.

"He won't be paid alright!" Viola cried through the kitchen casement window which opened onto the backyard. The window slammed right back against the wall, the steel arm making more noise as it slapped the window frame.

Dillon lowered his head and hurried more. The two heads stayed at the windows until the sound of the barrow tearing at the gravel died away, and there was the angry clang of it hitting the tray of Dillon's lorry, and the sound of the spade and fork and clippers tipped from it sliding away to the edge. Dillon moved so fast the slide was barely finished before he was at the wheel, the roar of the engine setting up a great trembling of the bonnet.

"Where did that brick land, Pet?" Viola cried. "Did you see?" Petula had the better eyesight of the two.

Petula looked quizzical rather than vacant.

"What brick, Vi?"

"The brick he threw. I threw. Never mind. Go and see to the stove!"

She came out of the house and went close to the rose beds to peer into them. Then shook her head.

"Pet! Come and help me find where it came from. I want to put it back."

Petula's feet were on the stairs, trying to remember why. Then they made a rush to the back door. The day was cold and Petula held a handful of her cardigan to her throat. "Vi! We won't have him back!"

"He would destroy our Papa's garden!" Vi said, and went and sat on the seat that faced the beds. Petula sat beside her with the points of her shoes in the grass. Vi's big feet gripped and flattened it.

They used to sit there on Wednesday afternoons when Dr Alexander Holmes was visiting. He closed his surgery one half day a week, along with other business and professional men of the town, including Mr Parker who was the solicitor. Dr Holmes ate midday dinner with the Parkers. There was a great flurry to have it ready at one o'clock and the house cleaned, and depending on the season and the elements, vases of roses wherever Dr Holmes was likely to look.

Mr Parker brought him in the front way, so there were roses on the hall table, and more on the little shelf of the hall stand where he hung his coat and hat, and since you could see into the sitting room from there still more filled vases were on the end of the chiffonier, the round table in front of the fireplace and the centre of the mantlepiece. In case he put his head through the door and pointed it towards the french doors opening onto the veranda, the flap of the writing bureau was lowered to take the squat brass urn of short-stemmed buds.

Viola and Petula took turns at doing the flowers for Dr Holmes. The other helped Mrs Parker get the dinner.

"By Jove eh!" Dr Holmes would say at the sight of the roses. When he reached the dining room and saw the shine on the silverware and the white tablecloth and ser- viettes shining too with starch, and a single rose from Mr Parker's choicest bush in a crystal vase in the centre of the table he said "By Jove eh!" and rubbed his hands together. The girls, holding the chair backs to pull them out for Dr Holmes and their father, felt like roses themselves, nodding bright heads above the stems of their green velvet dresses, uncurling their petals in the warmth of Dr Holmes's praise.

He mostly said "By Jove eh!" once more when the dinner was brought in, Mrs Parker with the joint and the girls with platters of baked pumpkin and potato and Yorkshire puddings puffed up inside their skins. He often thought of saying the girls' arms of the same pale gold colour were so like the puddings they should take care he didn't take to them with his knife and fork, but Mr Parker, being a stern parent, might not consider it a joke in good taste.

One day he almost said "By Jove eh!" when his plate was about to be laid at his place, and went quite hot with embarrassment for the arms were not those of Viola or Petula but Mrs Parker. Dr Holmes saw them, white and tender as the potato that crumbled at the touch of his knife, and when they stayed close to him he realised they were waiting for his thanks, and he raised his eyes to the face, even smoother and whiter, two drop teeth showing

their tips fanned on the lower lip. Dr Holmes, moisten-
ing his own lips, thought of meeting their hardness, and
stirred his feet to release a hardness in his lower body.
Mr Parker coughed with a very straight back and the
girls fluttered, sure they were somehow at fault.

"Oh, dear me," Mrs Parker murmured and turned her
back to pull down the sleeves of her mauve silk blouse,
rolled up in the heat and forgotten in her hurry to get the
gravy to the table while it was still on the boil. Dr
Holmes loved dark, smooth, very hot gravy.

"What is your mother's first name?" Dr Holmes asked
Viola and Petula on the seat watching Mr Parker look
for aphids on the rose bushes.

Mrs Parker had pegged the washed tea towels used for
the meal on the line, then hurried inside as if she had
committed a breach of etiquette like undressing in the
open.

Viola and Petula knew their mother's name, but since
their father rarely used it, felt Dr Holmes should not be
told. Petula looked to Viola, charging her with the
responsibility of replying, but this responsibility was
lifted when Mrs Parker (never having done so before)
came out with a light cane chair and her sewing. She
looked up at the fluttering tea towels with an expression
that said How did you get there? Even after unrolling
the serviette that held her embroidery she stared at it as
if uncertain of what came next, and Viola came across to
her and looked at it over her shoulder, ready to help.
But Mrs Parker lifted a shoulder to dismiss her. She
took up her needle only to stick it back in the linen
straight away and made her hands into two fists
underneath it, so that the flower she was working on

seemed raised above the cloth as if a real flower had been dropped on her lap.

Of course, Dr Holmes said to himself, her name's Rose.

After he had gone home to the house he shared with his mother, the front veranda of which had been closed in for the surgery, Viola noticed Mrs Parker in her pantry rubbing glycerine into her hands. Her face went pink and she capped the bottle quickly.

"My sewing keeps catching on my skin," she said, threading the fingers of one hand in the fingers of the other, rolling the hands one over the other, pushing the skin down on the spread fingers. Viola saw the hands change, gain strength in the knuckles, their pinkness lightening and when Mrs Parker put the glycerine bottle back with the vanilla and lemon essences and cochineal she looked at them with a new respect.

Upstairs, Mrs Parker only partly closed her bedroom door to try on her new black shawl with the deep fringe and the embroidered peacock taking up the whole of the back part. Viola watched her mother tip her head to one side and lay her fair cheek in a black fold. She went to her and pulled some strands of hair loose from their bun to rest like spun sugar coloured pale gold on a fold too.

"Oh, no!" Mrs Parker cried, allowing the shawl to fall to the floor, using both hands to tighten the bun, poking at loose strands of hair as if they were shameful underthings not to be seen.

"Your father might need help!" she said, and gathering up the shawl folded it loosely, keeping her eyes from it and the mirror as she shut it away in the big bottom drawer of the wardrobe.

Viola went to her room with its view of the back garden and saw her mother standing close to her father, almost pressing against him, the two half bodies rising above the rose bushes, but Mr Parker was looking over the beds at the house as if he was thinking that's where she should be and he was waiting a respectable time for her to go, and if she didn't he would tell her to.

Viola and Petula were on the seat the next Sunday, Petula waving her boots gently above the grass, while they both watched Mrs Parker look for young beans in the vine over the fence. Mr Parker was cutting dead roses from the bushes and tossing them with the points of his clippers onto the bricks.

"Mumma is hoping there will be new beans for Wednesday," Petula said dreamily.

"Aren't you Mumma?" she called out, and Mr Parker frowned and snipped the air above a full blown rose.

"Ladies speak in low voices always, don't they Papa?" Viola said. Papa snipped a full-blown rose from its stem and Viola winced.

Viola suggested that for a change Mumma do the roses and she and Petula get the dinner for Mr Holmes on Wednesday. Viola watched Mumma's face, saw it trying to decide which would bring the greater pleasure to Dr Holmes.

"I don't know," she said, shaking her head and starting up the stairs.

"Mumma is sad but tomorrow's Wednesday," Petula said, shaking hers too.

When the girls came down for breakfast Mumma was serving Papa with a big plate of bacon and all the flower vases were missing, making the house seem terribly empty. Viola was drawn to the wash house where the smell of roses was heavy. There were the vases, the brass and crystal sending out little shafts of light and drawing them back again like someone breathing. The roses had settled down, stopped trembling under Mumma's hands, stopped their preening. They were so still they might have been wax.

Mumma had put all the yellows together, all the whites on their own, all the pinks by themselves, all the reds in the long necked porcelain jug with real gold trimming on the handle and little raised rosebuds also of gold in clusters where the jug was fattest.

Petula came to stand right behind Viola, breathing her words onto Viola's neck. "It will be terrible if Dr Holmes doesn't notice."

But he couldn't help it. Mrs Parker put the red roses on the hall table and the rush of air from outside when the door was opened sent them nodding a welcome and one very large one laid its petals back like hair flattened in a wind. Mrs Parker was there to meet him, her lace collar flung up against her cheek before Mr Parker shut the big front door. Dr Holmes said "By Jove eh," with his eyes above the hat he held ready to hang up. Then the fine eyes travelled all the way down the hall to rest on Viola, on her way into the dining room carrying a decanter of ginger wine which she set by Dr Holmes's glass, then turned the single yellow rose around on its stem to face his place.

Dr Holmes called at Mr Parker's office on a Saturday about a month later to say, providing Mr Parker raised no objection, he would court Viola.

"A very fine young lady," he said, swinging his hat gently between his knees, his eyes on the floor rug, a small smile starting up at the sight of the weights in neat little felt bags stitched to the corners to stop them from curling, which he could see they were doing with gentle stubbornness.

Those are her stitches I'm sure, he thought with terrible sadness.

Viola in Petula's bedroom flung her arms around her sister and swung her out as if they were in some wild dance.

"Think of it, Pet! Oh, think of it! I won't have to go to those dances any more!"

They parted with big backward steps from each other as Mrs Parker's feet whispered past the closed door towards the stairs.

The engagement was celebrated at one of the Wednesday dinners.

A sixth place at the table was set for Will Crean, fresh from University and a newly engaged assistant to Mr Parker. It was already decided he was a suitable match for Pet.

Mrs Parker was very good throughout the meal. She showed the tips of her teeth when Dr Holmes praised the beans. "The last of the crop," she murmured and put a small fork in her mouth with her eyes down.

"Oh, Mumma!" Viola said after the washing up, rubbing a slice of lemon left from the fish over her hands. "I can't believe I'll have a husband!"

Mumma put a chin on her apron top and untied the strings at the back. "That's sensible."

"Mumma?"

She went to the pantry to hang the apron there. "You mightn't have one either."

Viola went to the dining room and neatened the pile of pattern books there with a pile of pale blue muslin, returned to the table after it was cleared of the dinner things. She buried a hand in the fabric as if there was a danger of it flying off. Through the window she saw her father, fists on his hips, on the brick path where it was widest in the centre of the rose beds.

"I'll go to Papa," Viola said, pinning the muslin down with the scissors.

Mrs Parker put her chin up and showed the points of her teeth then more of them, curling her lips back so far.

"There's no hurry for it," Viola said, slipping with surprising gentleness on her big feet past her mother across the back veranda. She looked back then down to step with care onto the grass. "Years and years of time, Mumma."

Papa heard and came with a question on his face and sat on the seat and Viola sat beside him. Her left hand with the ruby ring lay on her grey tussore silk lap. Papa looked as if he might hold it, but turned his face so that his profile disappeared. Mumma came out to pull old overlarge beans, curled and ugly as deformed limbs, from the vine to half fill a bucket.

They watched her take the path through the roses to the fowl pens. The excited squawk of the fowls was soon lowered to near silence, an occasional scraping of a throat.

"Poor fowls," Viola said. "There's not much nourishment in dry old beans."

Petula was back now after walking with Will to Mrs Butterworth's boarding house, posting a letter on the way to relatives in Victoria, a sister of Mr Parker with a family of unmarried daughters, telling them of Viola's engagement.

Petula took a skipping rope from a nail on the wash house wall and went to the end of the brick path and skipped with a flurry of her skirt and a beating of her brown boots between bricks and rope. She slowed down and ran skipping onto the grass to make way for Mumma returning swinging the bucket. Then she skipped back, skipping with an energy that threatened to send the bricks flying with the rope. Papa was thinking he should tell her to put the rope away, she would be a young matron soon, when the bucket fell with a great clang and Mumma ran into the rope with an arm out and fingers groping to grasp it. She pulled it from Petula and gestured for her to pass and ran quite a way down the path into the roses. Mumma began to skip quite wildly with Viola and Petula about to scream to her that the rope was too close to the roses, when Mumma moved to the edge of the bricks and skipped even harder and wilder with the rope tearing the roses from their stems, the petals flying about like confetti and Mumma's face pink as the deepest pink with the teeth showing and the eyes lowered, although directed at the seat where Papa and Viola were. Petula stood on the lawn by the upturned bucket with feet apart and fists buried into her weeping eyes.

Mumma moved farther down the path near the big bush of reds and soon the air was filled with the flaying pieces, like velvet chopped with ruthless scissors. Or pieces of bloodied flesh.

Viola pulled at Papa's arm to pull his eyes from the sight. She was surprised when her cheek touched his shoulder to feel the warmth of his flesh when her own was chilled.

"I'll never leave you Papa," she whispered.